The

OF IT ALL 3

BESTSELLING AUTHOR

TAMYRA GRIFFIN

The Point of It All 3
-Written By-
Tamyra Griffin

Copyright © 2016 by True Glory Publications
Published by True Glory Publications
Join our Mailing List by texting TrueGlory to
64600 or click here http://optin.mobiniti.com/V2Y

Facebook: **Author Tamyra Griffin**

*This novel is a work of fiction. Any resemblances to
actual events, real people, living or dead,
organizations, establishments or locales are products
of the author's imagination. Other names,
characters, places, and incidents are used fictitiously.*

Cover Design: Dottie Dzigns
Editor: Tamyra L. Griffin

Acknowledgements

To my readers; I can't thank you enough for supporting me and reading The Point Of It All series. Being a published author is a dream come true for me and your support is what keeps me going.

I also need to thank again Shameek Speight. You have single handedly made one of my dreams come true. Even three books in, I still can't believe I'm here.

I need to thank my family for their love and support; as well as anyone that liked, shared or talked about my books. Thank you so much.

Even though I've thanked you previously, to my best friend of thirty-nine years. You have been a tremendous help, and have made this 'author life' as you call it, so much easier on me. Thank you for your encouragement, support and for being my biggest cheerleader.

Happy Reading, Tamyra xoxox

Table Of Contents

Prologue

D sat back holding his new daughter and watching all the people he loved back together in the same room. Today was the day they released Destiny from the hospital and Kiko came home with little KJ. Even being surrounded by love, he had a nagging feeling about who the snake may be. Almost sure he had it all figured out, a sneaky grin came across his face. Kissing Destiny, he got up to place her in her bassinet and joined his family. Not wanting to return to their home, they were staying at a house D rented an hour away.

"Aiight now. You keep holding her and her all spoiled, you're gonna be up with her in the middle of the night."

"My baby girl is aiight."

"I can't be baby girl anymore?" Kaliah asked.

"You'll always be my baby girl. Now I have two.... you and your sister."

"Okay." She perked, leaving out the kitchen.

"How you feeling ma? You okay?" D asked, rubbing Orchid's back.

"I'm good daddy." She cooed, kissing him.

"Aiight now. You know you gotta wait that six weeks dawg. You setting yourself up for failure."

Laying in the bed waiting for Orchid to climb in, he pulled her close, placing kisses on her neck. Ever since they'd gotten her back, he hasn't let her out of his sight. There was still that nagging feeling in his gut that let him know the drama had only just begun.

"What you thinking about?" Orchid asked turning to look in his eyes.

"How blessed a nigga is to have you and our kids."

"And....."

"Just thinking a few things over.... nothing major."

"I know your ass like the back of my hand. You're thinking about the same shit I've been thinking about. I don't feel secure knowing someone close to us, maybe even someone we call family, is a cross artist. At first I thought it was Shelle."

"How do you know it's not?"

"You're not the only one with eyes for hire nigga. Looks like she's on the straight and narrow like she said, so I don't think it's her."

"Check you out. I appreciate that ma, but the only thing I want you to do is take care of home. Let me handle the rest. Aiight?"

"Yeah......I guess I can do that. After I beat your old hoe's ass now that I'm not pregnant. Her ass was talking real greasy when they had me."

"Fuck her. I fucked with her because she was convenient. You know my heart belongs to you."

"It better."

"You know I gotta bounce for a few days right?"

"D, just leave it alone for now."

"I can't do that ma. I'm not trying to have my family constantly looking over their shoulders. They kidnapped you and held you fuckin' hostage. I can't let that go ma."

"Is there anything I can say or do to make you change your mind?"

"You can damn sure try but nah. I gotta do

this."

"Just make sure you come back to us."

"I ain't going nowhere. 'Til death do us part and your man don't plan on dyin' no time soon."

"Again."

"I'm never gonna live that shit down."

"Damn right."

"I love your ass."

"I love you too D."

D kissed Orchid's forehead and slipped out of their bedroom. Stopping in to kiss his kids, he left out to meet up with Keon and the rest of the crew before hopping a plane to Puerto Rico. 'Cut of the head and the body dies." D thought as he drove to the airport. Firing up a blunt, he turned on the radio to get his mind off of Orchid. "Ain't that a bitch." he said with a smile as Anthony Hamilton crooned 'The Point of It All'. After the song ended, he turned on some Notorious BIG and morphed into murder mode.

Stepping out the truck with his hood over his eyes, he was in murder mode. Dapping up Keon, Boz and a couple more of his trusted soldiers, he was ready to roll.

"You good?" Keon asked.

"I'm good. Let's do this."

Knowing Javier had a hellified surveillance system, D knew there was no way they'd get into the house undetected; so he planned on walking up to the front door and ringing the fucking bell. Before he could touch the bell, the door swung open and Ramon stood wearing a smirk. Extended his arm to signal him in, D stepped into the house, watching him closely.

"Took you long enough. We were expecting you."

"So that means you've been doing all the shit on your bucket list......like getting some pussy."

"Stupid niggas like you never know when to shut your mouth. You're lucky I didn't help myself to some of that sweet, pregnant pussy." He said with a laugh. "You've got a beautiful wife. What does she see in you?"

"She recognizes my gangsta. Where this nigga Javier? I ain't got all night."

"You fuckin' right."

Javier's bitch ass was in his office, watering his plants when they walked through his office door. He looked at his robe and chuckled because it was similar to the robe Keon was now always riding him about.

"Something funny?"

"Yeah, your robe."

"Have a seat."

"Nah, I'm good. Who the fuck is this nigga you got planted and what the fuck does my wife have to do with any of this shit?"

"Damonte, Damonte. You always did think too highly of yourself. You're only a small piece of the puzzle. You all were. The bottom line is; I want my money. Your wife was just a casualty of war. Well, she would've been had you not found her. As far as my partner you befriended......I think I'll keep that to myself. If you were as smart as you thought you were, you would've figured it out. Guess you'll never know."

D heard a gun cock behind him and thought

'Fuck!" Waiting to feel the familiar burn of a bullet entering his body, he saw a beam go up his chest and land between Javier's eyes before he felt a bullet fly past his face.

"Puta!" Ramon barked before he fired off a shot.

Dropping to the floor hoping he'd dodge the bullet, he felt it tear through his arm. "Ugh fuck!" he gritted, grabbing for his gun. Ramon got off another shot before he caught him in the chest two slugs. Taking a step, Ramon finally dropped to the ground before he heard another shot.

"Nigga get your ass up! It's your arm, not your dick." Keon cracked, reaching out his hand to help him up with his good arm."

"Shit still fuckin' hurt.

"Bring your bitch ass on. It's mu'fuckas upstairs, I don't know how many though."

"Kill anybody you run into...but save that bitch for me. I got something for that ass."

Creeping around the corner towards the stairs, thy were greeted by gunshots. Ducking for cover on the sides on the stairwell, D putt his gun through the staircase, he fired up the stairs. "Ugh!" they heard before seeing a man in black stumbled down a few stairs and attempt to scurry back up. Keon fired his whole clip up the stairs and into his back. Seeing a shadow, D fired up the stairs again.

"Don't shoot!'

"Bitch, bring your ass down here now!" D hollered, recognizing Esmerelda's voice. "Drop your gun down the stairs."

Seeing the Tiffany blue and chrome gun come

down the stairs, he ordered her down. She walked slowly down with her hands behind her back. Once she got close to them, D noticed her fidgeting behind her back. Firing a shot into her arm, Esmerelda fell down the rest of the stairs.

"Damn dog. Why you ain't just kill her?"

"Nah, that's too easy for this bitter bitch. Help me get her into the kitchen onto the table."

Tying his wrists and ankles to the drawer handles of the island, D grabbed the wooden block that held butcher knives and the sharpening stone.

"Nigga, what the fuck you about to do?" Keon hissed as he watched her rip off her dress.

"Just some minor surgery." Said with a far off gaze in his eyes as he sharpened a large blade.

"I ain't trying to be here for that shit. I'mma go find Boz and them. Hurry that shit up. Crazy mu'fucka." Keon said as he walked out the door shaking his head.

"Looks like your ass got lucky. I was gonna get real medieval on your ass but......I gotta go. Any last words?"

"Yeah....... hurry home."

With that D plunged the knife into her chest and twisted. "See you in hell bitch."

After finishing an L in the truck with Keon, he dapped him up and headed into the house. All he wanted to do was kiss his heads, take a hot shower and lay up under his wife.

After stopping in Lil D's room, D went to check in on Kaliah until her heard Destiny fussing. "Here I come baby girl." He said heading into the hallway bathroom to wash his hands. "Aiight, what's wrong with daddy's precious…… "

"Baby girl's sure a precious. I know first-hand."

"What the fuck………"

Chapter 1

"Hold your fire playboy. We wouldn't want anything to happen to little mama; now would we?" the unknown fuck boy said.

Noticing he held a gun in the same hand he rubbed his daughter's back caused D to see red. Taking a deep breath in an attempt to stay calm, he spoke calmly.

"Who the fuck are you; and how the hell you get in my house?" D asked through gritted teeth, his gun still aiming at his head.

"I have my ways. Don't shoot the messenger my nigga."

"Yeah? What message you got for me."

"King Rah just wanted you to see how easy it is for him to reach out and touch everything and everyone you love."

"Aiight, you delivered your message. Get the fuck out my crib."

"You funny." The unknown said and chuckled. "What guarantees do I have that you won't put a bullet in my head as soon as I turn to walk outta here? Nah, lil mama gonna take a walk with us." He said, lifting a still sleeping Destiny from her crib.

"D, if you wake this…..... Who the fuck is this?"

"Damn! Yo, you're finer than I heard. You's a lucky nigga. Had I known you had all that laying up in your bed, that would've been my first stop."

"Who the fuck are you; and why do you have my child?"

"O, go back in the bedroom. I got this."

"D…."

"O, carry your ass back in the room……now!"

"Maybe we'll see each other again under different circumstances ma." He said blowing her a kiss.

"Fuck you." O spat, reluctantly walking out of the room.

"Feisty and fine! You got good taste my nigga. Now be a gentleman and walk me to the door."

Stepping to the side slowly, D moved to allow him out the bedroom door. Never taking his gun off of him, he followed closely to the front door.

"Cherish your family, you never know when they could be taken away."

"I hear you. Now give me my……" he began before he was punched in the face and Destiny was shoved into his arms before the "messenger" took off running.

Holding Destiny close in one arm, D let off shots with the other; hoping to a least wound him.

"Fuck!" he shouted, scaring Destiny; who'd slept through the commotion. "I'm sorry lil ma." He said softly, bouncing her in his arms.

"D! Oh my God! Was that gun shots?! Is Destiny okay?"

"She's fine. Take her and go back upstairs." He ordered, pulling out his cell.

"If you're calling Keon, I did that already. He's on his way. Are you gonna tell me what the fuck is going on and why a strange nigga was in my house; holding my daughter?"

"O, I'm not doing this shit with your right now. Take your ass upstairs and pack some shit up for you and the kids."

"I am not leaving my house until…..."

"Do what the fuck I said Orchid! Damn!"

Without another word, she turned to go up the stairs. Stopping to look back, she watched as he paced back and forth like a caged lion. *This shit is not gonna turn out good at all.*

After getting Destiny back to sleep and in her bassinet next to their bed, O dialed Kiko; hoping she might be able to shed some light on things.

"Shit, I was about to call you to find out what the hell was going on."

"The hell if I know. All I know is I heard voices over the monitor and when I walked into Destiny's room, this nigga has my baby; and guns were drawn. Then D's ass gonna banish me upstairs like I'm some damn kid."

"Listen at your ass. I bet you over there pouting too." Kiko cracked.

"Kiss my ass."

"Just give him some time to calm down."

"Yeah, I guess. Let me finish packing and see what Daddy has for me to do next."

"When you find something out, call me back."

"I got you."

"Whoa nigga!" Keon yelled as he walked up to the porched and D took aim at his head.

"My bad."

"Where O? Her and the kids straight?"

"Her hard headed ass upstairs packing."

"You know how she is. So, what this nigga say?"

"Shit. Said this King Rah pussy wanted me to know how easily he can touch everything I love. This nigga got me all the way fucked up right now."

"True that. I'mma get Boz and them on it."

"Anybody associated with this nigga, bring they asses in. If this nigga fuckin' farts, I wanna know about that shit."

"That shit's nasty, but I'm on it."

"I'mma get O and the kids settled, then I wanna meet with everybody. This nigga needs to die asap! This nigga had a gun on my baby girls back!"

"I know that shit's fuckin with you bruh. Go upstairs and talk to your wife though. Hit me as soon as y'all settled."

Once she had the kids settled and they'd finally gone back to sleep, Orchid joined D in the bedroom of the suite they were occupying for the night. He still hadn't said too much of anything to her since they'd left the house, which was fine by her; being as though he pissed her off.

"You wanna tell me what that was all about now?"

"I ain't got nothing to tell you O." he said non-chalantly, while pulling on a blunt.

"So you're trying to tell me this random ass nigga decides to stop by to hold our daughter in the middle of the night, uninvited and holding a gun mind you; and you know nothing?"

"The nigga Rah sent him aiight! That's all I got for you right now."

"So what now?"

"I'm getting you and the kids settled someplace safe until this shit is handled."

"Settled where? Damonte I know you don't think I'm gonna relocate my family because of this bullshit."

"I know you're gonna relocate because I just told your ass that's what the fuck you doin'. This shit is not up for discussion."

"Nigga......I know you're stressed right now, but I highly suggest you watch how you talk to me. I let that shit at the house slide, but you got me twisted if you're gonna take your frustrations out on me!"

So pissed off she didn't want to be in the same room as him, Orchid grabbed a pillow and blanket before heading to the living; slamming the door behind her.

"This nigga got me all the way fucked up." She huffed before finally getting comfortable on the couch and allowing sleep to find her.

Chapter 2

Relocating definitely had Orchid in her feelings but, her best friend and her family coming along made it a little easier to handle. Like herself, Kiko was not feeling having to uproot her family; so she and Keon weren't on the best of terms either.

Orchid sat on Kiko's bed as she handed Keon his ass as he left out of the bedroom and finished packing her last few essentials. She hadn't heard from D all morning, and she damn sure wasn't going to bed the first to bend; especially when his ass was in the wrong.

"Y'all worse than me and D." O cracked.

"I can't stand his big black ass. He makes me sick."

"You know you love that man's dirty drawers."

"Depends on which day you ask. Today, damn sure ain't one of this days."

"Orchid! Yo get your ass down here right now!"

"Is that Khalil?" O asked, not sure if she was hearing correctly.

"O, I know you fuckin' hear me."

"Oh, this nigga done lost his damn mind." Kiko perked, storming out of the bedroom before she could.

"Why must every negro in my life test me right now?"

By the time Orchid got downstairs, Kiko was already standing in front of him going in; complete with the angry black woman neck roll and hand on her hip.

"Khalil what is the problem; and who the hell do you think you're talking to like that?" O spat.

"More importantly, how the fuck you gonna come up in my crib and act fool? You done lost your damn mind. O you better get this nigga." Kiko fussed as she walked towards the back of the house.

"When were you gonna tell me you were taking my daughter away? And where the fuck are y'all going?"

"First, you need to watch how you speak to me. I was gonna tell you...."

"When? When y'all got to wherever the fuck y'all were going? And your ass still ain't said where that was."

"I can't Khalil."

"Why; because your fuckin' husband said so? Huh?" he gritted a little too close to her face than she cared for.

"Khalil…..."

"Nah, fuck that! This nigga comes back from the dead, fucking everything up and you chose him; I let that shit slide. I even agreed to letting my daughter live in the same house with this nigga while y'all play house and shit. You not taking my daughter no fuckin' where Orchid. I love you but there will be some shit between us about my seed."

"I'm gonna walk away from this conversation before I say something I regret."

"I'm not done talking to your ass!" he said grabbing her arm, pulling her towards him. "Go get my fuckin' daughter…...NOW!" he barked in her face.

Orchid's eyes widened, but not because of his yelling. Hearing a gun cock close to his head, he slowly let her arm go.

"Nigga, you will lose your life fuckin' with that one right there. Fuck with me if you want to."

"You know what they say about pulling a gun on a nigga."

"All too well. The only reason I haven't bust a cap in your ass is on the strength of your daughter. Don't fuckin' tempt me."

"Fuck all that. This is between me and O. That's my fuckin' child."

"Nah, this is between you and me now. You done fucked up your privileges, now everything goes through me. O got upstairs, get the kids and get in the car."

"D......"

"This shit ain't up for debate. Go get the kids and get your ass in the car."

Turning to head for the stairs, Orchid's blood was boiling. In all the time they'd been together D had never talked to her the way he had been; and the shit wasn't sitting well with her. *I'll cuss his ass out later when he's not holding that damn gun. Crazy nigga.* She thought, as she began to climb the stairs.

"O, we need to talk about this shit!" Khali yelled behind her.

"You don't fuckin' listen do you? You don't address her. You wanna talk, you do it through me."

"You know this shit ain't over."

"Not by a long shot nigga."

"DADDY!!!" Khaliah yelled, running down the stairs and jumping into his arms. "We're going on an airplane."

"Yeah, I know. How about when you get back you and Daddy go on a plane ride together."

"Can we go see Mickey and Minnie again?"

"We can go anywhere you want lil mama. I love you."

"I love you too Daddy."

"Khalil! Wsup man?!" Lil D perked, walking over to dap him up.

"Damn you getting tall. I can't call you Lil man no more."

"I'm trying to do a lil somethin'. I wanna play on the basketball team this year."

"You'll make it. When you have your first game, hit me up; I'll be there."

"Cool. Talk to you soon."

"Aiight Lil man." He said dapping him up again with a smile on his face.

Orchid gave him one last look before she walked out the door behind the kids holding Destiny. The smile he had when dealing with the kids was a thing of the past and was replaced with a serious mean mug.

"You look like you're in your feelings playboy. You got something you wanna say?" D asked, his hand still on his gun.

"You know what.... we'll save this shit for another day." Khalil said moving towards the door.

"As a matter of fact, we won't. I need some answers about a few things and you have them; so have you might as well get comfortable for a spell."

Chapter 3

The beauty of their temporary home distracted Orchid from how pissed off she was that she even had to relocate. After getting Destiny down for her nap and making sure Kaliah and D were good, she stepped out onto the balcony of her bedroom to fire up a much needed L. She and D hadn't spoken a word to each other since they'd left Keon and Kiko's. Part of her was saddened at where they were presently but the majority was pissed. Even before he left them there at the house, he only addressed he kids; as if she did something wrong.

"Where you at girl?!" Kiko yelled as she walked into her bedroom.

"Out here."

"A blunt to the face?! Yeah, you definitely in your feelings." Kiko said sitting in a lounger next to her. "Sharing is caring; pass that here and light this one."

"I see great minds think alike."

"And you know this!" she perked, mimicking Smokey. "Y'all still not speaking?"

"No. He's giving me the silent treatment like all of this is my fault."

"Just give him some time ma. He's stressed and worried about his family. All his needs is some time to cool down."

"To hell with all that. He done went from talking to me like he's lost his damn mind to not talking to me at all. Shit, this is my family too; and he acts like I'm not supposed to ask questions. Hell, he ain't telling me nada, so of course I'm gonna ask."

"Both of y'all stubborn as hell."

"Aren't you one to talk."

"Unlike you two bull headed asses, Keon and I talked. You know he wasn't leaving me for God knows how long and not put in that work first."

"You only folded because you wanted some dick."

"No! Well, that might have been part of it; but that's not the point."

"Get the fuck outta here." O cracked up laughing, damn near choking on the smoke she held in.

"Girl I couldn't resist. This way that dick was sitting in them basketball shorts moving and just staring at me; it was calling me."

"Saying what?"

"Kiko......put the jaws on me."

"I can't stand your ass!"

"So y'all talk?" Keon asked, pouring them shots of Henny.

"Yeah I talked to that nigga."

"Not Khalil; your wife nigga."

"Nah, she ain't had shit to say to a nigga."

"And who's fault is that?"

"Hers."

"Nah nigga, this one's on you."

"How you figure?"

"She worried about her family…...and your black ass. Her biggest fear is losing you again. Shit, I'd think something is wrong with her ass if she didn't ask questions. You know her ass is stubborn, hard headed, nosey…...."

"Don't be goin' in on my sweet angel." D cracked.

"Sweet angel my ass! That shit comes in spurts."

"Shit, you should talk. You married to Satan's lil sister."

"And you have his other sister." Keon cracked and touched his glass to D's. "On some real shit though, you need to talk to her. You don't know how all this shit is gonna play out; the last thing you want is for something to happen and y'all fucked up."

"True. You talk to Kiko?"

"Hell yeah! A nigga swallowed his pride, put on my hard hat and handled some construction before we rolled out."

"Construction? What the fuck is you talking about?"

"Demolition work my nigga. I tore down walls before I left out that piece."

"You wild for that." D cracked. "Yeah, you right. I'mma talk to her after we handle this lil bit of business Boz got for me."

"Oh yeah. You just better make sure you handle your business with sis. A happy wife makes a happy life."

"True that. Hit Boz up, let him know we in the air and I need him to bring my tools to the spot."

"Here you go with this Jeffery Dahmer bullshit."

"I'm about to make that nigga look like a boy scout."

As soon as they hit the ground, they headed to the warehouse where Boz was waiting for them to arrive. Banging twice on the door, Boz swung it up with a smile on his face.

"My niggas." He said, dapping them up.

"What's good with you cuz? Good job on this here." Keon said walking towards the table where there was a man bound.

"Anything for fam."

"You bring my tools?" D asked, ready to get started.

"Yeah. I got everything you asked for."

"Aiight. Let's do this; I got shit to do." D said approaching the table. "Who do we have here?"

"Basseem; one of Rah's lieutenant's." Boz answered while lighting a cigarette.

"So Basseem, where your man's at?"

"Probably in your wife's pussy nigga." He spat.

"Is that right?" D perked, wearing an evil grin.

"Yeah mu'fucka. You might as well go 'head and shot me, 'cause I ain't tellin you shit."

"Shoot you?! Why would I do something like that? Nah, I have something else in mind."

"Aw shit. Here we fuckin' go." Keon said shaking his head. D had developed a twisted appreciation for the art of fileting niggas since his stint as a hit man. Even with an iron stomach like his, some of the shit he'd see him do made his shit turn.

"The other night I was laid up with my wife watching some crazy shit on the Learning Channel. They were draining the fluid from this niggas lungs to save his life. In your case it'll be the opposite; but you get my meaning." D said as he pulled on a pair of latex gloves.

"I'd talk if I were you. The shit that's about to go done is nothin' nice." Keon said shaking his head.

"Man fuck y'all niggas."

"Suit yourself."

"Aiight then; where's my shit? Ahh." D said picking up a scalpel. "First they made an incision right along here." He said jabbing the instrument into his side, then pulling the blade down.

"Awww shit!" Boz yelled covering his mouth.

"Nigga you better not throw up in here. That's DNA evidence mu'fucka!" Keon barked.

"Fuck man! I don't know nothin'! Fuck!" Basseem yelled, moving around trying to escape his restraints.

"That shit hurt, don't it?" D asked, picking up a spreader.

"What you gonna do with that shit?" Basseem yelled, his eyes bulging out his head.

"I gotta spread your ribs to get to your lungs. What you think?"

"Man fuck y'all niggas. Just shoot my ass."

"This nigga got balls." Boz cracked.

"We'll see about that." D said as he approached him again.

Putting the spreader into the incision, he wedged it between his ribs and pulled on the handles.

"Arrrrggggggg! Fuck man!" he yelled out in agony. "Aiight! Aiight! I'll tell you what I know."

"That's more like it. Spill nigga." Keon gritted. "Who is this nigga?"

"He owns a club up top called Oasis. All the officers meet up there once a month. Last I heard he lived up there somewhere. Only his higher ups know where that is."

"Who are his high ups?"

"Suol and Kadeem. You already met Suol."

"How the fuck I meet Suol?" D asked.

"He was the nigga that came to your house."

"So what do you do? All you do is run the trap?" Keon asked.

"Come on man! I already told you what I know."

"You ain't answer my question nigga."

"I followed your wife man. Come on man." He cried.

"I guess I was wrong about them balls huh?" Boz cracked.

"Who's fuckin' wife you follow nigga?" Keon barked.

"They had me follow your family man. Come on man, please!"

"Mu'fucka!" Keon barked before punching him in the same ribs D had spread open and exposed.

"Damn! That shit sound like it hurt!" D cracked. "Anything else we need to know?"

"Yeah.... all your niggas gonna die fuckin' with Rah. Go 'head and kill me, I'm dead already."

"Say no more my nigga." Keon gritted before using his body for target practice.

"Damn my nigga! I ain't even get to the good part of the surgery."

"Do what you want with that nigga. We got what we needed." Keon said coolly, taking the L from Boz and inhaling deeply. "What's next?"

"After we finished here, I'm getting on a plane and going to kiss some ass. Happy wife, happy life right."

"My nigga."

Chapter 4

It was close to two in the morning when D and Keon arrived back to the house. After smoking an L on the deck, D dapped Keon up before heading back into the house. "Put that hard hat on my nigga." Keon said before he headed up the stairs.

Covering Destiny up, he kissed her forehead before heading into Kaliah's room. Her body hanging half off the bed, he slowly placed her legs back into the bed, kissed her forehead also and left out to go to D's room.

"It's almost two in the morning, what you still doing up?"

"Wsup Dad? Mom said I can stay up. You come back to make up with mom?"

"What you know about that?"

"I can see mom's not happy; and she said "He needs to get his life together. He got me twisted!" Lil D impersonated his mom causing D to crack up.

"You wild for that. She really said that?"

"Yeah. If y'all making up, I need to request a lil brother this time. It's too many women running around here."

"I feel you on that. Don't you stay up too late. I'm gonna holla at your mom."

"Alright Pops. Don't forget, we want a boy."

"You handle that video game, leave the grown folks business to your pops. I got this. Make sure you turn off that tv before you go to sleep."

"I got you Dad. Love you."

"I love you too."

Easing the bedroom door open, D crept into the room and undressed. Standing next to the bed, he admired his sleeping wife. Even with no make-up and her hair in a messy ponytail, she was still the most beautiful woman he'd ever seen. He smiled seeing that she was sleeping in his t-shirt, even though he knew she was pissed with him.

"You just gonna stand there and stare at me all night?" Orchid mumbled sleepily.

"You're beautiful, I can't help it."

"Unh huh." She mumbled and turned over.

"Can we talk O?"

"Can't it wait until the morning?"

"Nah, it can't. I don't want to go another night with us like this ma; I can't. Turn over and talk to me."

"What is it Damonte?" she huffed, turning over and sitting up. Even though she wanted to slap the shit out of him, her husband was fine.

"I can't be D now?"

"Not when you waking me up at two in the morning."

"Look ma…...I owe you an apology."

"A few."

"Aiight, you can get that. You're my wife, my better half; and I shouldn't have tripped on you the way I have been. Seeing that nigga in our house standing over Destiny, this whole situation with this nigga got me tripping and I took that out on you."

"Yeah. Your ass was real reckless at the mouth and disrespectful."

"I know ma; and I apologize for that too. I know you worried and you wanna know what's going on but I need for you to focus on taking care of our family and let me handle this shit."

"Handling family means handling your ass too. I have no problem with sitting back, letting you handle the gutter shit; but still need to know what's going on with my husband. I've been beat, kidnapped, almost raped; I'm a lot stronger than you think. My biggest fear is losing you again; and you not coming back this time. That I can't handle."

"Ma, you're never gonna have to worry about losing me; I promise you that. And I promise not to keep you in the dark again."

"Or talk to me like you've lost your damn mind. Next time you might catch a beat down. Your wife got a mean right my nigga."

"I don't want no problems." D cracked and laughed. "I love you; with everything in me ma."

"I love you too D." she moaned, leaning forward to kiss his lips.

"Damn I missed those lips." He moaned as he laid her back on the bed.

Pulling her panties down her legs, D licked his lips as her neatly shaved pussy stared back at him. Kissing his way up her leg, he spread her butter soft thighs and lapped slowly at her center causing her to moan. O ran her hands over his soft waves as he sucked feverishly on her clit; moaning, "Suck that shit daddy! Damn!" Lifting her legs, D began fucking her with his long tongue until her felt her body shiver and she bust her first nut.

"Come ride daddy's face. I want all them juices sliding down my throat." He moaned licking his lips as she assumed his favorite position.

Slowly riding his face as she sucked and slurped on his center, O could no longer resist putting the jaws on the glistening dick staring at her. Stopping to suck on the head as if she was nursing, O then moved slowly down his dick until he touched the back of her throat. "Aww fuck ma!" D moaned out, muffled by her juicy folds. Bobbing up and down on his dick while massaging his balls, O sucked and moaned until she felt him pulsing in her mouth. "D…damn! You trying to do a nigga in! Fuck!" he moaned as he toes twitched and all he could do was palm her ass as he felt his nut rise from what felt like his toes until he was painting her tonsils. Even once he came, still sucked him back to life and kept going.

"Oh word?! Your ass ain't the only one that can do some shit. Stay that ass still." He ordered, holding her in place as he began flicking his tongue in and out of her opening.

"Ohhhh shit daddy! Mmmm." She moaned as he continued his clitoral assault.

Licking up to her ass, D reached around to play with her clit, causing her moans to escalate. When her ass started moaning gibberish, he knew he had her ass and a grin spread across his face. When he felt her legs shaking and her pussy tightened around his tongue, he applied more pressure to her clit. With her moans now screams of pleasure, he went in for the kill. In a matter of seconds, he felt her juices hitting the back of his throat and glazing his lips.

"Yeah. That's what daddy wanted. You gonna handle this dick for daddy?"

"I…I need a minute babe." Orchid moaned, out of breath.

"Nah ma. Daddy ain't had none of his pussy in a minute and I ain't waiting no more. Turn that ass over." He ordered; grabbing her by the legs and flipping her onto her stomach. "Unh! Look at Daddy's juicy pussy right there!" he moaned playing in her wetness before watching his dick disappear inside of her.

"Oh….my God daddy! Damn!" Orchid damn near yelled as he drilled into her with long strokes.

"Damn I love this…...pussy. Shit ma! I love you."

"I love you too daddy. Mmmm shit!" she moaned as he ground deep into her center, losing himself in her silky folds.

The sun was coming up when D finally allowed Orchid to tap out and get some sleep. Moving a stray hair from her face he stared at the woman he was lucky to call his wife. Kissing her forehead, he pulled her close and let sleep find him.

Chapter 5

Rolling over and looking at his cell, D saw it was a little after one in the afternoon. Turning back over, he saw Orchid was still knocked out sleep with his ass cocked in his direction. Unable to resist, he moved her leg and slid up inside of her slowly.

"Mmm. What…. are you doing?" O moaned sleepily.

"Sliding this dick up in you; starting my day off with a bang." He moaned as he slowly stroked her.

"Come on babe, I'm…...tired."

"Unh huh."

Once he started hitting that spot, all her protests went out the window and she was trying to escape the dick. Leaving her laying limp in the bed, D got up to shower before checking on the kids.

Seeing the kids were straight, D headed into the kitchen to hook he and Orchid some lunch. Walking through the door, he came face to face with Kiko sitting at the island mean mugging him.

"What I do?"

"Besides keeping my ass up with all that noise coming from your bedroom."

"I was handling some construction."

"What the fuck? Construction?"

"Don't act like you don't know about them walls being tore down. I did a lil construction of my own last night." Keon cracked, walking in and moving to kiss her forehead. "That's right my nigga, put that hard hat on." He perked, dapping D up."

"Y'all are assholes. Since you brought your black ass back here to fix shit, I'll allow it."

"Damn, am I married to you too?"

"You better thank your lucky stars for that too."

"You can hardly handle one of me; ain't that right babe?" O added, coming into the kitchen and hugging him from behind.

"I think I handled you quite well last night….and this morning." D moaned, turning to kiss her.

"Aiight! That's enough of that shit. Let's go out back and burn this tree right quick. Let her ass breathe."

"Love you daddy."

"I love you too ma." He said leaving out the sliding door.

"You keep it up and your ass gonna end up pregnant."

"The devil is a lie. Right after Destiny was born I had them give me the birth control shot when he ass wasn't around. We hadn't even left the hospital and he was talking about having a son."

"Oh no you didn't! You better not let him find out about it. He's gonna put his entire foot in your ass."

"Who you telling? That's why I did it when he wasn't around."

"Girl…...I'm gonna pray for your ass."

With his mind right, having patched things up Orchid, D was back in murder mode and their next stop was New York. Checking into the Marriot for a quick shower and to change, they headed to Club Oasis hoping to catch this nigga Rah. Stashing guns they hoped to get inside, they exited the car headed to the entrance.

"Aiight my nigga. Anything look suspect, we shoot first and ask questions later." D stated.

"You ain't get to tell me. You got your shit on?"

"I'm good my nigga. You?"

"Most def."

"Aiight. I made a promise to my wife and yours I intend on keeping."

They got to the front door and were pat down by lax ass security who didn't find either of the guns they were packing. Moving slowly through the club they took note of the exits and different rooms. Dapping Keon up and heading to the other end of the bar, D ordered a bottle of Hennessey to pass the time. Drinking straight from the bottle, he felt a tap on his shoulder. Turning around, he took in a fake ass Ving Rhames looking nigga in a tight as suit.

"What up?" D asked, looking at him like he was small.

"The owner wants to see you and your partner upstairs."

"I'll be up there in a minute."

"This ain't a request. Now follow me."

"You really shouldn't flex in that suit like that homie, you already look like you about to bust up outta that shit." D cracked nodding at Keon, who got up to follow.

Following their big for no reason escort down a hall, he led them to an elevator that they took two floors up. Leading them into a plush office, he waved them over to two chairs that sat in front of a desk. The nigga on the other side sat in an oversized chair with his back towards them talking on the phone like his ass was The Claw from Inspector Gadget or some shit.

"You have a call?" he said handing the Ving wanna be the phone.

"Who the fuck is this?" D gritted into the phone.

"Is that anyway to greet an old friend?"

"Old friend? Miss me with the bullshit."

"It's Qua Styles. Long time no see nigga."

"That's for good reason. What up with you and what you need to speak with me for."

"Seems we got a little issue. I hear you looking for my partner Rah."

"Yeah and?"

"You fuck with my partner, that's fuckin' with my paper. I can't have that. Now, if we were to come to some type of agreement, I might be able to help you out."

"What agreement is that?"

"First, there's the small matter of a territorial issue. Thanks to you niggas shooting shit up, I'm losing money in y'all neck of the woods. Let my men set up shop without any interference."

"And?"

"I got some unresolved business I need to handle with your Byron. I need you to arrange a sit down. If we can get those two things handled, I'm inclined to give you Rah's location. We got a deal?"

"Nigga, who you think you fuckin with? You think I'm gonna do that shit for you to fuck me over?"

"Come on D, I thought we were better than that. Aiight, let's get this sit down poppin and I got you. Matter of fact, bring Orchid with you; we could use a lil eye candy."

"Really nigga? You can fuck around and be on the same hit list as your man fuckin' with mine."

"Don't be like that my nigga. Just wanted to say hi to an old friend. Hit me up when it's set." He said ending the call.

Homebody that once sat with his back towards them finally turned around to face them, tossing a business card across the desk with his miniature hands.

"Now get the fuck out." He said, waving them away.

"No wonder you got this big, buff supa negro. Damn my nigga!" Keon cracked at his small stature.

"Fuck you." He attempted to bark holding up a short, pudgy little finger.

"Yo, my daughter would love to have one of you in her play room." He continued cracking. "Yo these niggas wild."

Chapter 6

"Well lookey here! My favorite son in law." Theresa perked, hugging D.

"Shit, I better be your only son in law." D cracked. "How you doing Mama T? You still sexy as hell."

"You know, gotta make it do what it do. I got a new husband to keep happy." She perked. "I know your big ass ain't standing over there trying to act all quiet. You better come hug my neck."

"How you doin Mama?" Keon asked, picking he up in a bear hug.

"I'm always good. This is a nice surprise. It's nice to see you two. What brings you to my neck of the woods."

"I need to talk to B."

"Well, he and Wendell went to the store to grab a couple of things I needed for dinner. Get comfortable, they should be back soon."

"Ma T, you got some brown for your boy?" Keon asked.

"You know I do. Help yourself. So, can I ask what this is all about?"

"I need to ask him about one of his old people's. You recognize the name Quadee Styles?"

"That dirty... Yes, I know the name all too well. Keon, you better pour me one of those too; looks like I'm gonna need it."

Catching Mama T up on what they'd learned so far and what D cared to share, he anxiously waited for Byron to return. Hearing the alarm charm and the front door open, they heard them heading towards the kitchen.

"Oh shit! Look what the wind blew in!" Byron perked, shaking hands with D before pulling him into a brotherly before doing the same with Keon.

"You looking good B. How you been?" Keon asked, checking him out looking like new money

"I'm good. How's my sisters and the kids?"

"They good, driving both our asses crazy." D cracked.

"They here? Where they at?"

"Nah, we here alone. They're someplace safe."

"Someplace safe. What the fuck is going on now?"

"I need you to tell me about this nigga Quadee."

"Styles?"

"Yeah."

"Where the fuck y'all dig this nigga up from?"

"This nigga dug himself up. This nigga is asking for a sit down with you; and I need to know what's up. Shit ain't adding up."

"Aiight. Me and this nigga go way back…....."

Fourteen Years Earlier….

"Wsup Q? B ran out right quick but he's on his way back. You can come in and wait." Orchid perked, walking back to the couch where she had been posted up.

Qua watched her plump ass and hips move in the little shorts she wore, licking his lips. Sitting on the couch across from her, he couldn't help but take in her curves.

"So wsup with you ma?"

"Just chillin'; hanging around the crib for now."

"Nah, what up with you? You grew up to be real fine. How come we never hooked up?"

"Because you're like the brother I never wanted."

"So, you never thought about us?" he asked, lifting her leg and sitting them on is lap. "So you really ain't feeling me?" he asked rubbing on her legs.

"No, I haven't. Q, quit playing."

"Does this feel like I'm playing?" he asked, sticking his hand in her shorts and swiping her clit.

"Q, stop."

"Oh, so you one of those cock teases, huh? I got something for your ass." He gritted back slapping her."

"No! Q, stop." O yelled, fighting him off.

"Keep your ass still." He barked before sending his fist into her mouth.

Sitting up slowly, Orchid touched her mouth to see that she was bleeding; until he started clawing at her shorts as she screamed. Hitting her with another back hand that robbed her of the little bit of fight she had left in her, Orchid laid on the couch and cried as he freed his dick from his pants. Squeezing her eyes and thighs tight, she prepared for the worst.

"What the fuck?!" B yelled, walking in and snatching Qua off of Orchid. "You…. done…. fucked…. with…...the…...wrong…...one!" He barked in between stomps to ribs. Pulling out his gun, he shot him in his knees.

Leaving him on the floor bleeding on his mom's cream carpet, B went over to check on Orchid. Still on the couch with her eyes close, she began to swing at him.

"O, it's me. It's B; it's okay."

She finally opened her eyes and the tears began to slide down her cheeks. Grabbing the blanket from the back of the couch, he draped it around a shaking Orchid.

"Go up to your room and don't come down until I come get you. Okay?" he asked, getting no response. "O, go up to your room; now ma. Go 'head."

Blinking her eyes, what he'd said finally registered and she started towards the stairs.

Turing his attention back to Qua, Byron pulled another gun from the small of his back and cocked it.

"So, you a rapist huh? You was gonna fucking rape my sister; in our fuckin' house?"

"Man, she wanted that shit. C'mon B, we better than this."

"Nigga, we ain't shit!" were that last words Byron needed to speak before he sent a bullet into his chest.

"FREEZE! DROP THE WEAPON NOW!" an officer yelled, his gunned aimed at Byron's head.

Complying with the officer's orders, Byron dropped the gun and then fell to his knees. The officer held him at gun point while another cuffed him. Two more officers rushed through the door and over to Qua who laid on the floor gasping for air with blood coming from his mouth. As medics prepped to remove a barely alive Q from the house, B was pulled to his feet.

"NO! What are you doing?!" Orchid yelled, running down the stairs with blood still staining her face and wrapped in the same blanket Byron covered her with.

"O, it's gonna be okay. Call Mom, let her know what happened."

"Ma'am, do you need medical attention?" a female officer asked.

"No, I'm fine. Did you get him?"

"Get who ma'am?"

"Q."

"Well…...what do we have here?" An overweight, pink over asked smugly as he held a duffle bag filled with weight.

"That mu'fucka!"

Byron received twelve years for the weight Qua planted, attempted murder and conspiracy; which was added to his charges after Qua recovered from injuries and decided to turn witness, giving up information on spots his father ran that were now his. With Byron and his dad out of the way, their territory was Qua's for the taking; which is exactly what he wanted.

Present Day….

"That coward ass pussy! No wonder he asked for Orchid to be at the sit down!" D raged.

"Hell nah! Keep Orchid as far away from him as possible. His ass had a sick fixation with her; who knows what his ass is capable of now."

"His ass ain't gonna be capable of shit when that ass is filled with slugs." Keon said with a clinched jaw after hearing the story.

"So who was this nigga working with?" D asked, trying to piece shit together.

"At first we thought it was Javier's brother but, he can't be a partner to shit dead; we never figured that shit out."

"Well, there might be someone we can get the answers from. Javier's brother Robert has a twin; who from last I heard is still alive, barely."

"Ma you think you can get in touch with him?" D asked, ready to hop on the plane to go hold his wife.

"It may take me a little time, but I'll work on it."

"Thank you. I love you for that." He said and kissed her cheek. "Sorry to drink and run, but I need to go see about my wife."

"So when we doing this sit down? I got some unresolved issues with this nigga."

"I'm with the fam for a couple days. After I leave there, we'll meet up and go handle this nigga. You better hope you get your hands on him before I do."

"I feel you bruh." B said, embracing him in another brotherly hug. "Tell my big head ass sister and the sister I never wanted I said I love them; kiss the kids for me."

"No doubt. Love you Mama T." D perked

"I love you too; and you Keon, drinking all my shot."

"You know I got you when you come visit."

"You better; or that's your ass!"

Walking quietly into the kitchen of the villa, D stood against the kitchen door watching as his fine ass wife moved around the kitchen in a sexy black one piece and sarong. He already loved her to life but having heard what she'd been threw when she was younger, he wanted to hold her tight and never let go.

"Shit! You scared the hell outta me. Why didn't you say something?" Orchid perked.

"Can't a nigga just stand back and appreciate looking at his sexy ass wife?"

"By all means." She cooed, walking into his open arms; kissing him deeply.

"You know I love you with everything I am right?"

"Yes; and I love you daddy."

"You and our kids are the best part of me. Having a beautiful, strong woman like you by my side as my rib, let's me know I did something right in this life."

"Is everything okay?"

"It will be. Where's the kids?"

"They all went to the store with Kiko. Where's Keon?"

"In the bathroom. You know that nigga can't stand all the flying. That nigga got bad guts like Craig's daddy. On some real shit, come holla at me for a minute." D said taking her hand, leading her to the living room.

Orchid sat on the couch wondering what the hell was going on, when he sat in front of her on the coffee table and took her hands in his.

"I talked to Quadee."

"Qua.... how do you know him?" she asked, her face displaying a mixture of pain and rage.

"We used to do some business back in the day. I was at a club trying to find this King Rah nigga and he scoped us out. Had security take us to the office and this nigga was on the phone; asking for a sit down with B."

"No! You can't let that happen!"

"Calm down ma, please." He said softly, stroking her hand. "I flew down to Florida and already talked with B and Mama. Ma, B told me about what he did to you." He said and looked into her eyes that were now filling with tears. "You don't have to talk about it if you don't want to."

"If B told you what happened, there's nothing left to tell. D, I don't want him anywhere near me or my family."

"You don't have to every worry about that. Although that shit happened before me, I'm gonna handle that nigga for hurting; that's my word."

"Baby, he's a snake; the foulest kind of nigga. Keep your eyes on him at all times."

"I'm already on it. You good though?"

"I'm good. Better now that you're here. Oh.... I need to go back home. I have a doctor's appointment."

"It's too risky. Why can't you go to the doctors here?"

"They don't have the medicine I need."

"What medicine? You good?" he asked concerned.

"Yeah, it's……my birth control shot." O mumbled.

"Say that again. I don't think I heard you right."

"It's my birth control shot."

"Since when you start getting that shit?"

"I've only gotten it once; right after Destiny was born."

"Why you ain't talk to me about that shit?"

"All you wanted to talk about was "having a son ASAP!" she mocked him. "I wasn't ready for that."

"You don't want to have any more of my kids?"

"I do baby; I just didn't want to have another baby until Destiny was at least one. You weren't hearing that."

"Aiight, aiight. I'll let you get that; but you ain't getting that shit no more. Understood?"

"Yes Daddy." She cooed.

"Your ass ain't slick, you know what you doing with that shit. Carry all that ass up the stairs so daddy can get his fix. Just for you doing the bullshit, I'm putting in extra work and getting your ass twice as pregnant."

Chapter 7

"What up my nigga?! How was vacation?" Qua perked, flipping onto the couch in the living room of the suite he'd just walked into.

"It was cool; until I had to come back early because of the fuck-up ass niggas I got working for me." Rah gritted. "Y'all find this nigga and his family yet?"

"Nah, it's like they dropped off the face of the planet. We got eyes on his and his boys house and it look they packed up."

"Get everybody together, I wanna meet up tomorrow night at the spot. And where the fuck Basseem ass been?"

"I'on even know. I been hitting this nigga up for the past few days and ain't got no answer. It don't look like the nigga been home either. I was gonna go past his trifling ass BM's crib to see if he been over there."

"Yeah, so that. Watch out for her scandalous ass. She'll talk her way onto your dick and hit you in your pockets. You fuck with her; you better strap up twice; ain't no telling what's living up in that pussy."

"I ain't even on her ass like that, but I got you."

"Hit me when you know something."

"Aiight."

"Oh, wsup with that sit down?"

"I'm waiting to hear back from them niggas at any time."

"Let me know when that shit goes down. Now get the fuck out. I need a shower and a nap. Y'all niggas make a nigga fuckin' tired."

Pulling up around the projects, Qua parked his car, tucked his gun and headed to Bassem's BM apartment.

Hearing loud music coming from the other side of the door, he banged a couple of times before he heard, "Who the fuck is it?! Banging on my damn door like that."

"It's Qua. Shut the fuck up and open the door!"

"Oh. What up Qua, come on in." She cooed, standing back to allow him to walk in past her.

Tanaysha was a scandalous ass hoe but she had ass for days, a tiny waist and titties that stood up tall and made a nigga take time out to admire them. Reluctantly, he looked back at her ass in the tiny shorts she wore before tossing a dirty shirt out of his way and sat down.

"So, what brings your fine ass to my neck of the woods."

"I'm looking for Bas, you seen him?"

"No; and when you find his ass tell him I'm looking for him. Rent is due and BJ need sneakers."

"When the last time you talked to him?" he asked, peeling off two hundreds to hand to her.

"Thank you boo." She cooed, leaning over to kiss his cheek; titties damn near spilling out of her tank top. "It's been almost a week since I talked to him. You know me and Bas don't fuck with each other like that; haven't in a while."

"I heard."

"So, wsup with me and you? I've been digging you for a minute now."

"Bas is like fam ma. He ain't gonna like that shit."

"Well…." She began, dropping to her knees in between his legs. "…. what Bas don't know, won't hurt him." She moaned as she unzipped his jeans, reaching in and pulling out his dick. "Damn nigga."

"You like that shit huh? You know what to do with all the beef?"

"Oh, I can show you better than I can tell you." She moaned and began licking him from balls to head.

"Oh shit." Qua moaned.

BOOM!

"What the fuck was that?!" she asked, head popping up with the quickness.

"Go check that shit out. Pass this in front of the peep hole first." He said passing her a take-out menu from the coffee table before grabbing his gun and then his pants.

"Who is it?!" Tanaysha yelled.

Getting no response, she opened the door slowly. Peeking out, she saw a box sitting in front of her door. Picking it up, she brought it in the house and sat it on the coffee table.

"Nobody was out there; just this box." she said looking at him as she opened it.

Opening the bag inside of the box, a strange smell hit her. Looking a little closer, she began to scream at the top of her lungs. Looking inside the box, Qua saw an arm with a tattoo he knew without a doubt was one Baseem wore exposed proudly.

"What the fuck?!

Cocking his gun, Qua headed out the front door hoping to catch whoever had just made delivery. Looking around frantically, he saw no signs of anyone attempting to make an escape. Seeing nothing out of the ordinary, he went back inside to tend to Tanaysha; who's cries he could hear outside.

Sitting in a hooptie with tinted windows across the street from Tanaysha's apartment was Boz and Hak; cracking up laughing at Qua as he walked back into the house. Hitting speed dial, he put his phone up to his ear.

"What's good fam?"

"The package has been delivered."

"That's wsup. Was that nigga shitting bricks?"

"Yo D, you should've seen this niggas face. Shit was hilarious."

"That's wsup. Keep eyes on that nigga and everybody else we on. I'll meet up with y'all in the next day or two; I'm getting some QT in with the fam."

"That's wsup my nigga. Tell O I miss her cooking."

"I will. She hooking shit up now."

"Rubbing that shit in. Aiight my nigga, I'll holla later."

"Aiight. Good looking."

"What 's next?" Hak asked, passing Boz an L.

"We keep tabs on this nigga. Stacks and them got that, we on to something else my nigga."

"Fuck!" Rah barked, tossing his phone across the room after receiving the news about Basseem. Not only was he one of his captains, he was also his younger cousin. Pacing the room, inhaling a blunt in just a few pulls, his mind was working overtime. Stopping mid stride, he came to the summation that some may have been following Qua for them to know he'd be at Tanaysha's house at that time.

Looking around for his phone to call up Qua, he punched the phone upon finding it shattered into a few pieces. Snatching up his keys, he headed out of his suite to purchase a new phone.

"Niggas think they asses slick, but I got something for they ass."

Qua stood next to the door as their lieutenants, captains and Rah's right hand walked into the make shift conference room one behind the other. Since delivering the news of Basseem's death, Rah been on some other shit; and he wasn't looking forward to seeing him.

Once everyone was in the room, Qua took his seat as they waited for Rah to arrive. After sitting around talking shit for about a half hour, the phone in the conference room rang. Rah's right hand Kyrie gave Qua a smirk and answered using the speaker phone.

"Aiight, we all here."

"Listen up niggas. I'm getting real fuckin tired of the level of incompetence. Because of it, we lost a good soldier; my mu'fuckin cousin!" his voiced boomed through the phone before he paused. "From here on out, since niggas wanna act elementary, we adopting the buddy system 'round this bitch. Any pick-ups, two of y'all go. Nobody comes to my spot period! And watch your fuckin' backs; y'all may have tails on you. Until I figure shit out, I'm low profile. I'll see y'all when we do this sit down shit. Y will fill you in on the rest." He said and ended the call abruptly.

Qua sat quietly, in his feelings that all of a sudden shit seemed to go through Kyrie and he was supposed to be his partner. With nothing else to add to the meeting, he dapped everyone up and left out feeling like some shit wasn't quite right.

Chapter 8

With Kiko occupying the kids and D still sleeping, Orchid took the opportunity to take a hot bubble bath. Between the kids and D having her on her back every chance he got, she'd barely had a few moments to herself.

Docking her IPod, she let her robe hit the floor and slid into the hot soapy water. Leaning her head back, she closed her eyes as Faith Evans voice soothed her soul. Singing along with "Soon as I Get Home", she was interrupted by the feel of a leg entering the water and touching hers.

"Did I wake you?" she asked with her eyes still closed.

"Yes and no. I didn't feel you in the bed next to me. Sit up." D ordered, sliding behind her.

"Don't come up in here starting no shit."

"I came to take a bath with my wife, what you talking about; and how you gonna deny daddy? I got papers on this pussy." He said, putting his hand between her thighs; ribbing his fingers across her clit.

"Mmm. Stop. Fucking with you and your construction, I'll have no walls."

"Shit, daddy love them walls; and you love daddy in them. Don't you?" he said softly in her ear as he circled her clit.

"Mmhmmm."

"Nah, answer daddy." He moaned, applying pressure to her clit.

"Yes daddy. Yes."

"Come on ma, get your surf board on."

Straddling him with her back against his chest, Orchid slowly lowered herself onto his dick until he filled her up. Winding her hips slowly, she tossed her head back in pleasure as he gently pinched her clit, before slowly circling. Feeling her pussy contract, he knew she was about to bust her first nut.

"Yeah, give daddy all the juices." He moaned, circling faster as she picked up her pace. Damn ma, ride this dick. Fuck."

The sounds of moans and water splashing filled the bathroom, drowning out Faith's voice. Leaning her over the tub, D began stroking the pussy slow and deep, watching his dick disappear in her pink folds.

"Is this daddy's pussy; forever?"

"You…. know it….is."

"Tell me." He moaned picking up his pace, having no mercy on her spot."

"This is your pussy forever daddy. Damn baby." She moaned as she felt another orgasm coming on.

"Yeah, cum all over this…...."

"Mommy, my dad…...."

"Kaliah no!" Orchid shrieked, trying to shield her and D. "Tell him I'll call him right back. Wait for me downstairs."

"Mommy said she'll call you back. Her and Daddy D are in the bath." She heard her say on the way out.

"Shit. We might've mentally scarred her." O said shaking her head. "Can you take your dick outta me so I can wash and go handle this?"

"She gone now, let daddy get this nut. Get back in."

"If you plan on getting anything, you better hop your ass out before I get in this shower."

"Get that ass up on the counter." He ordered, coming towards her stroking his hard, wet dick.

After having her ass handed to her, Orchid showered on unsteady legs before leaving D in the shower to throw on some clothes and find Kaliah.

Finding Kaliah in the family room, she was still on the phone telling her Dad how much fun she was having in "Turkey Pesos". Chuckling silently, Orchid sat next to her kissing her forehead.

Kaliah, go play in your room while I talk to your daddy."

"Okay." She perked before running off.

"Hello."

"I'm glad you could hop off the dick long enough to have a conversation with the father of your child."

"Oh, you done definitely lost your damn mind nigga. You know firsthand I'm not gonna tolerate the disrespect. So, your ass can either apologize sincerely or we can end this call now; and we can try this again when you get your life together."

"Aiight. I apologize O. I'm just not feeling not seeing my seed. It's been over a month since I laid eyes on her; all because your fuckin husband decided it's best."

"He made a decision that was best for his family, which includes Kaliah. And you can chill with the disrespect, it's not his fault I chose him. If you wanna be mad at anyone, be mad I me."

"I can be mad at both y'all asses. His ass should've stayed dead."

"Apparently you've been smoking the same shit you're serving up. You can talk when you learn some act right; cause right now, it seems you done lost your yella ass mind. Yella niggas always got to be the ones to act the fuck up." O fussed as she ended the call.

She could understand his frustration at not seeing his daughter. One thing she could never question was his ability to be a good father and his love for Kaliah. However, this ignant, disrespectful side of Khalil was something she'd never experienced.

Walking into the bedroom still fussing to herself, D peeped the change in her mood. He laid on the bed in silence watching her curse and snatch things from her drawers that she was about to put on.

"What's wrong with you?"

"Nothing?"

"Don't nothing me. The kids are quiet and I know you can't be made at me after all those nuts you busted."

"Shut up." She perked, not wanting to laugh but giving in. "Khalil just pissed me off, that's all."

"He wants Khaliah?"

"He wants to see her but… Nothing, never mind. He misses his daughter."

"Nah, don't do that. What happened?"

"He just got disrespectful. I know he misses his daughter but he's outta pocket. I had to bang on his ass."

"What he say?"

"It doesn't matter. He apologized."

"If the apology was good enough, you would still be pissed. Apparently what he said got to you, so what he say?"

"It's not so much what he said, it's just how he said it. It's almost like he hates me."

"Stop stallin'. What he say?"

Reluctantly, Orchid repeated the things Khalil had said to her. As she talked, she could see the change in D's demeanor and a look of evil she didn't recognize. Seeing his jaw clinching, she regretted ever saying anything.

"Call his ass back."

"D, just let it go. He has a right to be a little angry."

"Fuck that! Ain't no nigga gonna disrespect you, not while my ass is around. I don't give a fuck who it is. Call his ass up."

"I'mma need you to calm down first."

"I'm not gonna calm down, so you might as well get this shit over with. His ass lucky I ain't in driving distance. You gone call him or what? Matter fact, I got the nigga's number."

"D...."

"Orchid, go somewhere with all that." He said sternly as he waited for him to pick up.

"What the fuck you callin' my shit for?"

"I'mma tell you this shit one fuckin' time. This is your last pass nigga. Now you disrespecting my wife?! I let your ass keep breathing 'cause you baby girl's pops but after today, that shit don't matter. Let me find out about one more fuckin' thing and I'm coming for you."

"I want to see my daughter. Since you seem to be callin' all the shots, you talk that shit over with your wife and get back to me." He said and ended the call. "This mu'fucka must've absorbed some fuckin' gamma rays or started smoking crack. He got me all kinds of fucked up." He spat.

"Bae, just calm down. It's your last night here with us, let's just enjoy it. Please."

"I'mma let you get that. We gonna work something out so this nigga can see baby girl. I'm telling you straight up ma, you 'bout to be short a baby daddy if he keep on with his bullshit."

"I don't think I will come to that, but I feel you." She said softly, straddling his lap as he sat in an oversized chair.

"Your ass think you slick; distracting a nigga with all this warm pussy on my lap."

"Is it working?"

"Fuck yeah."

Since it was Keon and D's last night in town, Orchid threw down in the kitchen; with little to no assistance from Kiko. As much as her ass watch the Food Network, her ass ain't picked up on any pointers. After Kiko finished the garden salad, the only thing she made her responsible for, O called everyone to the table to eat dinner. After blessing the table, they started digging in like the Klumps at the buffet.

"So Dad, how's it going with that lil brother we talked about?" Lil D asked.

"Boy! Ain't nobody having no lil brother no time soon. So whatever you and your dad got planned, forget about it." Orchid said, rolling he eyes at D.

"What?! He asked me about it." D said with a mouthful of food; trying not to laugh. "I'm working on that Lil man." D said about a whisper.

"Can I have a lil sister Mommy?" Keona asked.

"We can definitely work on that." Keon said, winking at her.

"The devil is a lie!" Kiko perked. "You see what your ass done started?" she said, tossing an Olive at D.

"You can't blame a brother for wanting to have a big family. It don't help that my wife got that...."

"Hey! Little Mr. Sex Education is sitting here." Orchid perked, smacking D.

"My bad. Keon, you talk to ya boy?"

"Yeah. We'll talk about that later though. That nigga trippin'."

After the kids ate their fill, they were excused from the table. Able to get into more adult topics, first up was Khalil. All though she had a bad feeling about it, Orchid reluctantly decided to allow Kaliah to go with her father for a week. She'd be leaving with D and Keon in the morning and meeting Khalil in New York to drop her off.

The next morning Orchid hugged and kissed bot her husband and Kaliah like it would be the last time she'd see them. Although she was only five, Orchid had gotten her a cell phone and taught her the passcode to get into it. If Khalil wanted to be an ass about letting her talk to her, she'd be able to call her phone. Giving her one last kiss, Orchid let Kaliah board the plane with Keon.

"Stop stressing ma, she'll only be gone a week; and I'll see you in two. Aiight?" he said, pulling her close and kissing her forehead before kissing her lips. "I love you......with everything I am."

"I love you more. You make sure you keep that promise."

"Most definitely. I'll call when she's with him. Go 'head home."

"Don't tell me what to do."

"You know you like it." He said, slapping her ass. "Fine ass."

Chapter 9

The first couple of days Kaliah was gone were hard but surprising, Khalil was cool about things whenever she called. Maybe him not seeing his daughter was the reason behind his change in behavior. Although they didn't have much to say to each other, they were cordial and then he'd pass the phone off to Kaliah. That was, until the third day.

Orchid called Khalil's phone that morning just as she had done the previous days. Getting no answer, she figured they might have been sleeping late or were out. Waiting until later that afternoon, she tried his phone again and got the same result.

"Girl, be easy. You know Khalil isn't gonna let anything happen to his daughter."

"I know that; that's not what I'm worried about."

"I'm sure they're just busy doing something. Come on out back so we can out something in the air. Your ass needs to calm your nerves."

"Maybe you're right."

After getting almost no sleep the night before, Orchid woke up and immediately reached for her cell. Dialing Khalil's number, she prayed he'd answer.

"What?!" he barked.

"What do you mean, what? I called all day yesterday and you didn't answer."

"Aiight, and? You don't need to call repeatedly to check up on her."

"I'm not checking up; I miss my daughter. I call to talk to her. I know you're she's good with you."

"I'm glad you said that. I'm not sure exactly what the fuck y'all got going on, but I think it's best that Kaliah stays with me."

"My child is not staying with you. When your week is up, she's coming back home."

"Nah, not this time. Not to mention, what kind of mom gives their five-year-old a cell phone."

"It's an emergency phone; and what do you mean what kind of mom? You know what, let me just speak to my daughter."

"Here, it's your mom." She heard him say to Kaliah before she heard her voice.

"Hey mommy. I miss you."

"I miss you too. Are you having fun with your dad?"

"Yup. I went to the park with my cousins and we went on the rides yesterday."

"That sounds fun. Did y'all take pictures."

"Yes. Daddy even put on Mickey eyes like me. D didn't eat all my fruit snacks, did he?"

"No, your fruit snacks are safe. Four more days you'll be home and they'll be here waiting for you okay?"

"Cool. Are you coming to get me or Daddy D?"

"I'm not sure but one of us will be there to pick you up. As soon as I talk to him to find out, I will let you know. You be good for your dad, okay?"

"I'm always good mom, duh?"

"You're right about that. I love you Kaliah."

"I love you too mom."

"Put your dad back on the phone. I'll take to you soon."

"Okay. Here daddy." She said and she could hear rustling as she passed him the phone.

"Yeah."

"I'll call you tomorrow so we can settle on her traveling arrangements."

"Yeah, aiight."

It was the night before Kaliah was supposed to return home and Orchid hadn't been able to get in contact with Khalil. His phone had been going straight to voicemail as well as the phone she'd given Kaliah. This particular morning, she got a recording saying his number was no longer in service. Finally losing it, she broke down.

"What's the matter?" Kiko rushed into her room and to her side.

"This mu'fucka took my baby, I know he did."

"Have you tried calling again?"

"It's saying his number is no longer in service. How could he?!" she yelled, now crying uncontrollably.

Kiko pulled her close and stroked her hair. Reaching for Orchid's cell while she held her, she dialed D's number.

"Wsup ma?" D answered with a man yelling in agony in the background. "I'm kinda in the middle of something."

"You might wanna get here.......asap."

"Kiko? What's going on?"

"Khalil took Kaliah."

"Hold on." He said before rustling could be heard. "Shut the fuck up! I'm on the phone." He barked at one of Rah's errand boys he was torturing. "Repeat what you said."

"Khalil took Kaliah. She hasn't been able to get in contact with him for three days; not his phone is not in service."

"This mu'fucka did what?!" he barked. "Where she at? Is that here I hear?" he asked, hearing her vomiting in the background.

"Yeah, hold on." She said, siting the phone on the bed to rub her back as she threw up into the trash can. "Can you talk?" she asked, getting only a nod.

"H…hello." She said between sobs.

"Ma, we gonna get her back. I put that on my life."

"D…. I know he took my baby. He said it was…...it was best for her to stay with him. I want her back." She said as she cried.

"I know ma. We gonna get her. I need you to try to calm down, I can't have you getting sick. I'm finishing up here and on the next thing smoking back to you. Aiight?"

"Yeah."

"Aiight, let me talk to Kiko."

"Yeah."

"Try to get her to calm down, we in the air in the next couple hours."

"I got her, just get your ass here."

"Yo, I put it on my life, your peoples is fuckin' dead!" D barked at Keon.

"Who?"

"Khalil. That nigga took Khaliah and had to have changed his number."

"No the fuck he didn't!" Keon belted, pulling out his phone to call him. Getting the same recording Orchid had been getting, he clinched his jaws.

While D finished pulling a niggas teeth out filling his veins with hypodermics of air, he called around to a few family members in New York. Getting the same story from a few of them, he dropped his head, dreading having to repeat the news he'd just heard.

"Anything?"

"They saying he brought a house somewhere down south a month ago, but no one knows exactly where."

"You gotta be fucking kidding me! Get Boz on the phone. Tell that nigga to put anybody we have freed up on racking this nigga down. A half mil to any nigga that brings me that pussy!"

Walking into the dark bedroom, dropped his back and walked over to the window seat where Orchid sat. Staring out at the ocean in almost as daze, she didn't realize he was there until he'd placed his arm around her. Turning to look at him, his heart broke as he stared into her tear filled eyes. Pulling her into him, she held on tight and sobbed while he held her. The harder she cried the more pissed he got. Not saying anything, he just held her until she cried herself to sleep. Not bother to remove her clothes, he carried her over to the bed, laid her down and covered her up.

Creeping out the bedroom, he stopped to take a deep breath and wipe the tear from the corner of his eye that threatened to fall. Going down the stairs, he passed by Keon and Kiko in the dining room; grabbing the bottle of Henny from the bar and headed out the deck. Popping the top, drinking straight from the bottle, D fired up his L and inhaled deeply.

"You good bruh?" Keon asked, stepping out back quietly.

"Do you know how much it hurt me to see her like that? All she did was cry until she finally fell asleep. That shit hurt me to my core." He said and stopped to drink from the bottle again. "I couldn't love you any more if my own mother birthed you; but if you got a problem with me offing this nigga, we got beef."

"The only thing we gonna beef over is you not sharing this bottle." Keon said standing next to him, taking a swig and handing him back the bottle. "Nigga you, O and them kids.......y'all my family. That nigga got my sister hurting, got you hurting; shit, all of us. Not only do I not have a problem with you offin' this nigga, I'm gonna help."

D didn't sleep but a few minutes throughout the night, staying up to watch Orchid. She even cried in her sleep for Kaliah. He loved Kaliah like his own, but there's no love like a mother's love; so he knew her pain was twice that of his if not more.

"Hey." She said sleepily, barely above a whisper as she turned to look at D.

"Hey. How you feeling? You need anything?"

"Besides my baby back? No."

"When the last time you ae something?"

"I don't know; a day or so maybe."

"We can't have that. Why don't you go shower and we'll go out to get something to eat?"

"I don't really feel like going out."

"Alright, we'll eat in." he said taking her hand. "We're gonna get her back; you know that right?"

"Yeah, I'm banking on it. Will you shower with me?"

"I'll run the water."

Washing Orchid from head to toe, D washed himself quickly before jumping out to help her out of the shower. Laying her on the bed, he rubbed her body down hoping to get her to relax a little. In the middle of her rub down, she'd fallen back to sleep. Throwing on a pair of linen shorts and wife better, D crept out to go get her something to eat.

"Where your ass going?" Kiko asked as he came through the kitchen.

"Getting her ass something to eat. Why you ain't tie her ass done and feed her?"

"Please, you know how her ass is. She's barely left that bedroom the last few days."

"This nigga say anything else last time she talked to him?"

"Just what you already now. I can't believe he would do some shit like this."

"Yeah well, his ass better enjoy his last few days on this earth with her because his days are numbered. Keep an eye on my babies?"

"You know I got 'em. Oh and D…."

"Yeah?"

"She's pregnant."

Chapter 10

Sitting behind the desk in the office of Club Oasis, Qua ran the night's take through the money counter before calling it the night. Since pretty much being downgraded to just a club owner, he was beyond salty at the situation; but he had big things in the works.

Hearing his office door open, he turned around in his chair with his gun in his hand, ready to shoot.

"What the hell you doing creepin' up on niggas?"

"Lil Wayne said it best, 'Real G's move in silence like lasagna'. That's the take for tonight?"

"Yeah. We did hella good tonight."

"Looks like it. I'mma need for you to get that sit down poppin' within the next week or two. I know that bitch nigga D gonna be there and I want his ass dead like yesterday. Every day this nigga is alive my ass itches."

"Aiight, I'll make contact. Anything else?"

"Yeah. Don't think I can't feel the heat coming off your ass whenever Kyrie is around. I'm grooming his ass so we can sit back and do nada but count money; so be easy."

"It's all good Rah."

"I thought you'd say that. Holla at me when you got the time in place."

"I got you."

Realizing he'd only given D his number to contact him, he hit up a mutual acquaintance to get his number, as well as some other information he hadn't previously been made privy to. "This dirty mu'fucka!" Qua perked after he ended his phone call and dialed D.

"Who the fuck is this?" D answered.

"Damn my nigga. I guess there really is no love between us no more, huh?"

"What the fuck you want and how you get this number?"

"You're not the only one who knows people. Anyway, listen up nigga. I want this sit down to take place within the next two weeks. Get in touch with Byron's bitch ass and get that shit worked."

"I thought you knew people. Why you ain't call him yourself?"

"Because some people are unreachable. Like I said, we get this sit down poppin', I'll give you what you need."

"That better be the case or that's your ass. I'll hit you when we ready."

"By the way, I was sorry to hear about your step-daughter." He said and ended the call.

"What the fuck you know about that? Hello?!" he barked. Looking at the phone, he realized he'd ended he call.

Calling back, he was sent straight to voicemail. "Something definitely ain't right with this shit." He said to himself while dialing Byron's number.

"Yo B. It's about that time my nigga.

Another week passed with Orchid in a depression. D would have to force her to eat, shower and even put clothes on. All she wanted to do was sit around in her pajamas and stare out the window. After trying everything he could, frustration began to set in and he had to step outside to put something in the air and get his mind right. He and Keon were leaving in a couple days and he knew if he wasn't there on her ass she'd only get worse.

"Still no change?" Kiko asked stepping out back behind him.

"Hell no and she's starting to piss me off. I know she's hurting, but damn. I miss lil mama too but she got other kids to think about and one she's carrying. I'm about ready to toss her ass up in a minute."

"That woman you married, as I'm sure you know by now, is stubborn as shit. The one thing I do know, the best way to motivate her ass, is to piss her off. We both know that's something you can do like no other."

"You know what…." He began and had to laugh. "I ain't even gonna argue your point."

"You can't. I'm going out to grab a few things. I'll take the kids with me so you can handle that."

"I appreciate you sis. What we do without you?"

"Crash and burn. Oh, I'll be expecting a nice, fat L of that goodness you and your boy been smoking on but his stingy ass won't share."

"I got you."

After finishing his L and making orchid some lunch that her ass was gonna eat, he climbed the stairs to the bedroom. Taking a deep breath, he walked into the room; prepared to piss her off like he'd never done before.

"Get your ass up."

"Leave me alone."

"Nah, sorry ma. I can't do that. Your ass ain't eating and you pregnant."

"Who's fault is that?"

"You wasn't talking all that fly shit when you were sliding up and down this dick, was you? Get your ass up and feed my baby."

"I am not in the mood. Now just leave me alone."

"You know what…....this pity party is over. You need to shake this shit off, this ain't helping Kaliah. I don't know who the fuck you are right now, I didn't marry no weak ass bitch! Are you my wife or not? Because this stank ass shell of a person sitting right here ain't the woman I married."

"Weak bitch?! Stank ass! Nigga, my child is missing! How the fuck did you think I'd feel? She's not your child, so of course you wouldn't understand."

"Don't you ever in your life say no shit like that to me again. Biologically she may not be mine, but I love her like she is. You think me, Lil D and everybody else around here ain't feeling some type of way? I've been in her life since she was one and you say some shit like that to me?! Fuck you O!"

"No, fuck you!" she yelled, walking up into his face before slapping him. Not expecting a slap back. "You mu'fucka! I hate you. I hate all this shit!" she yelled and broke down in his arms.

"I know you do ma…....and I'm sorry you have to go through this; all of it. I need you to snap out of this shit and fight back. This ain't you."

"You slapped….me." she said between sobs.

"You slapped me first; hard as hell too." He cracked. "I'd never put my hands on you but I needed to get through to you. I'm sorry." He said, looking into her eyes before kissing her.

"I'm sorry too; and I don't hate you. I love you with my entire being. This family is my everything."

"I know it is ma. Even though a big part of us is missing right now, we miss you. This kids miss you. I need you to dig deep and bring back out that feisty mu'fucka I married. Can you do that for me? I can't go out here and get shit done while I'm worried about you and my kids. I'm still pissed Kiko had to be the one to tell me you were pregnant too."

"I'm sorry daddy."

"Under the circumstances, I'mma give you a pass. We good?"

"Yeah. Pissing me off like that."

"Your best friend suggested it. Thank her for it."

"I definitely will."

"Aiight. Get your ass over here and eat. I'm gonna run you a bath, wash that rusty ass and you're coming out of this rum. This kids are starting to think you ran off some damn where."

"Yes sir!" she perked and saluted.

"Maybe I should slap your ass often; you come around quick."

"Whatever nigga." She said and waved him off as he walked away. "D?"

"Wsup ma?"

"Thank you."

"Anything for you ma."

"Mom!" Lil D perked, running to hug her. "You feel better?"

"Yes, much better. I'm sorry I haven't been here for you much. I love you very much."

"It's cool; I love you too. I know sometimes adults go through some things."

"Is that right?" she said and had to laugh.

"Yup." He said hugging her again before touching her stomach. "Can I name my new lil brother?"

"How do you know about the baby?"

"Dad said he'd be on it; and he's the man."

"Ain't that the truth." D chimed in, dapping him up.

"We gonna have a talk about this shit here."

"Okay, that's my cue to go. Can I go play my game?"

"Yes. I'll call you when dinner is ready."

"Well, look who came out of hibernation." Kiko said walking into the kitchen; carrying a sleeping Destiny in one hand and a shopping bag in the other.

"Yeah. Seems you little errand boy was quite effective." She said with a smirk, taking Destiny and cuddling her. "Thank you......for everything."

"You're welcome. I'm glad to see you up and about."

"Yeah. I thought your ass was a figment of my imagination." Keon cracked.

"Don't start your shit. You can get slapped too." Orchid cracked.

"Who else you slap?"

"She slapped the shit outta me my nigga. Had my shit stingin'." D said, rubbing his face at the memory.

"Damn. You let her Ike you?" Keon cracked before kissing her cheek. "Welcome back."

"Thanks. So who got a blunt for a sistuh?"

"Yo ass better not even think about it; and we got the doctors in the morning."

"Uh oh, here he goes with his militant maternity bullshit."

Laying with Orchid in his arms as she slept, he took in her beauty. Not one that was big on prayer, he had to thank God for bringing her into his life; and that he protects him and his family. No man pumped fear in put fear in his heart but walking into this situation with so many unknown variables, gave him cause for concern. Touching her still flat stomach that held their unborn child, he kissed her forehead before easing out of bed to the shower. They were due to take off in three hours to go scoop up Byron and then to New York for this sit down with Qua; and to hopefully get some information that would get him closer to his goal of laying this nigga Rah down, permanently.

Chapter 11

Having eyes still on Qua and confirming the location of the sit down D the window of opportunity they were looking for. Byron was to meet with Qua at an empty office space in the Soho area. Requesting he meet him alone, they knew Qua would probably have men posted around the building, knowing D and his crew wouldn't be too far behind. However, they had something else in mind.

Getting to New York a few hours ahead of schedule, D held an impromptu meeting with everyone that came up top. Having gotten the layout of the building, complete with HVAC plans and the whole shit, they were ready to execute their plan. With a little over an hour before they needed to move out to get in position, D called to check on Orchid and the kids.

"Yes, I'm fine and I'm eating." She answered.

"You better be; or that'd be your ass when I got back. How you feeling?"

"Pretty good, considering."

"I know ma; we gonna get her back soon. This fuck boy Qua mentioned her being missing when we last talked, so I think he may have some information about it. If he does, I'mma get it out of his ass tonight."

"Please be careful. You done knocked me up again, so I'mma need your help with all these kids we got."

"You couldn't get rid of me even if you tried. Even death, although that shit was staged, couldn't keep us apart. I'll always come back to you."

"You better. I love you daddy."

"I love you too O."

Sitting on the couch of his suite, L hanging from his lips, D looked over the plans to the building while checking in with Boz and the rest to the crew to make sure shit was in order. Hearing a knock at the door, he grabbed his gun, passing it in front of the peephole before opening the door.

"Took your ass long enough. You better not have no bitch up in here." Keon cracked as he walked into the living, taking a seat in front of the plans."

"Shit; and have O really kill my ass? Not worth is my nigga; I love my life."

"Yeah, it'd definitely be off with your head. You talk to her?"

"Yeah; you know I had to call and check on her. Make sure her and the baby was good so my mind can be right."

"I did the same. Yo Hak and them said they in place. Fuck boy only sent a couple niggas ahead and they got guns on them already. B straight?"

"He better be. I'm waiting for him to get here..." he stopped, hearing a knock at the door. "That might be him now." D said heading to the door.

"What up brotha-in-law? Y'all ready to do this?"

"Shit, you ready for this? Your ass is the one that's gonna be front and center with this nigga." Keon perked.

"Yeah, I'm as ready as I'll ever be. This shit has been a long time comin'. This nigga cost me over a decade of my life and violated my sister."

"This nigga did what?!" Keon barked.

"I'll fill you in bruh. B, just make sure you do whatever it is you need to get your ass outta there alive. I ain't trying to have to deal with your sister or Mama T; real talk. We got you on our end."

"Good looking. Thank y'all for this."

"We family; and this shit is bigger than just this niggas hard on for you." D clapped him up, pulling him into a brotherly hug.

"Aiight. Enough of this kumbaya shit. We got some niggas to kill."

"True that."

Despite Keon's getting stuck in the crawl space, they were in position in the crawlspace over the room where the meeting was to take place. D looked through the slits in the vent at Qua and some other big nigga he had standing next to him. Quietly opening the slits a little more, they listened in on their conversation.

"I wonder is this nigga really gonna show and if he bringing his fine ass sister." Qua said.

"What is it about this bitch I keep hearing about? Her ass must be fine as hell. Rah obsessed with her ass, your ass over here drooling over her… Let me know. You fuck her?"

"Not yet. I almost had her ass but she put up a fight. Her bitch ass brother came in and ruined my fun."

"Your ass ain't shit. You was just gonna take it?"

"Hell yeah I was. Her ass always had on these lil ass shorts walkin' 'round the crib and shit; and trust that ass is fat. I came at her on some real G shit and she pulled that "You're like my brother" shit. That shit pissed me off. Fuck it, I was young and shit."

"What you want with her now?"

"I was gonna take the pussy nigga. Not just because I want that shit. Her, her brothers, her bitch ass husband; all then niggas need to suffer. Watching me fuck his precious wife would kill that nigga D. What would really kill him is if her knew his wife had a…." he paused. "Come in!" he yelled at the knock at the door.

The nigga D immediately recognized as the nigga that was in his house walked through the door, with B bringing up the rear. Pushing him in his back towards the desk, he closed the door behind him. Pulling out his phone, D sent a text to Boz. **"The dark skinned nigga in the vest that just left out the office, keep his ass alive!"**

"B-eazy. Long time no see my nigga. Nice to see prison hasn't aged you much."

"I see outside life aged your ass; a lot. What the fuck you want this sit down for nigga?"

"The way I see it, me and you have some unfinished business."

"What business you got with me? Nigga you lucky your ass still breathing. If the cops hadn't come in and saved your ass, you wouldn't be."

"I ain't gonna front, you did a number on a nigga. Took me months to get my shit back right. I still walk with a fuckin' limp."

"Nigga fuck months. Since you like setting niggas up and turning snitch, I lose twelve years of my life you rapist ass nigga."

"You still bringing up old shit?" Qua asked and laughed. "Speaking of that lil incident, where's sis?"

"None of your fuckin business. What kind of real nigga stalks a female because she don't want his ass? You sitting behind that desk in your baggy jeans when you should be wearing a fuckin' skirt. You bitch made my nigga. Plotting on the next mu'fuckas shit because you too lazy to put the work in. You probably still the same ass kissing, bitch ass fuck boy you always been."

"Damn." Kyrie huffed and dropped his head, trying not to laugh.

"Fuck you nigga! Your ass ain't shit, never been shit."

"Is that why you wanted me out the way; so you could have the shit I ain't have?"

"Fuck you nigga. Where's the fuckin' money?"

"What money nigga?"

"You forget we were thick as thieves. I know you buried money before you went away and that should just about cover the expenses for me to start my new business venture."

"Is that why you asked me here? To again, try to take something somebody else put in work for so you can come up?"

"Nigga, I helped earn every bit of that money' so it's just as much mine as it is yours."

"That shit gone nigga. That was twelve fuckin' years ago. Even if I did have it, you wasn't getting that shit."

"I bet you'd give that shit up if I told you where to find Rah and your niece."

"Like I said, I ain't got none of that money; but how much you talking for the information."

"Since we go way back and figure in the friends and family......"

"Nigga get to the point."

"Let's say ten million."

"I'mma need to know what I'm paying for is legit information before I pass off anything. 675 West Breckenridge Drive, Reston Virginia."

"What is that?"

"That's the address to the house that nigga Rah just brought."

"Fuck is you doing yo?!" Kyrie barked, pulling his gun.

"Fuck that nigga Rah. His ass running around here playing the Godfather and shit, cutting out the niggas that helped make it where he is. Putting lil young ass niggas like you in the position to be handed shit that niggas like me put in work for."

"That's my uncle you talkin' 'bout mu'fucka!" Kyrie again barked and cocked his gun.

Before he could get a shot off at Qua, Keon hit him in the shoulder; causing him to drop his gun. Byron pulled his gun, letting off a shot a Qua hitting him in the shoulder, but not before taking a slug to the chest. Dropping out the ceiling like they were commandos, they stepped onto the desk; guns pointed at Qua and Kyrie.

"Well, well, well. Looks like we crashed the party." D cracked with a smirk.

"Yo ain't crash shit! I knew y'all pussies was gonna pull some kind of bullshit; which is why I got my niggas posted up around this bitch." Qua spat, holding his shoulder.

"Yo, bring 'em in." Keon said into his phone. Moments later Boz, Hak and the rest of the crew came in with the men he had posted up, with their hands zip tied behind their backs. "You mean these niggas?"

"Fuck." Qua mumbled.

"B! You straight?" D yelled, while keeping his eye on Qua and Kyrie.

"Yeah. That shit hurt like a mu'fucka though." He groaned, sitting up.

"Keon, light them niggas up; everybody except the late night creeper over there. Hit 'em with something painful and non-lethal."

"I got you." He said, busting shots without hesitation.

"Take these three niggas down to the basement. I got something special for they asses."

Having tied the niggas to the metal beams that where in the basement, D donned eyes that displayed nothing but pure evil and a grin to match. Nodding at Boz, he pulled his tools wrapped in a surgical apron out of a duffle bag.

"Here we go with this shit here." Keon said shaking his head.

"B, you might wanna head on out for the rest of this here." D said, pulling on latex gloves.

"What you gonna do with this nigga here?" he asked pointing at Qua.

"What you think?! I'm gonna kill his ass."

"I'mma need in on this shit."

"Suit yourself. I'll let you finish him off. Now, let's see." D said, picking up a long instrument that looked like tweezers. "We gonna need that bullet back." He said, digging the instrument into the bullet hole in his arm; Twisting and pinching until he pulled out the bullet. "So, you were planning on raping my wife? HUH?!" he barked, his voices echoing throughout the basement.

"Hell yeah. Fuck you and her nigga."

"Sounds like he got hate in his heart bruh." Keon added, lighting up a blunt.

"I firmly believe all rapists should have their dicks cut off and shoved down their throats; but we not gonna do that with you. Before we move forward, what were you gonna say about my wife nigga?"

"Fuck you. I hope that nigga kills all y'all; even your cock tease ass wife."

"Oh okay. Now your bitch ass wanna grow some balls huh? Too little too late my nigga."

Walking back over to his tools, he grabbed a small pair of forceps and surgical scissors. Without hesitation, he roughly grabbed his dick with the forceps and clipped his dick off with one snip of the scissors. Qua's screams of pain were agonizing and the sight of his unattached dick in the forceps had everyone in the room holding onto their shit for dear life.

"Wanting to rape somebody with this lil ass shit! Now you can kill his ass." D said to Byron who wore a look of shock and excitement.

While Byron used that nigga for target practice, he moved to his next victim; a nigga he's dreamed about killing every since that night he found him in Destiny's bedroom.

"If it isn't the messenger bitch. You like breaking into niggas homes, holding guns to they seeds nigga?! I've been dreaming up all kinds of ways to kill your ass since then and I still don't know what to do with your ass now that I have you in front of me."

"Come on man. I was just following orders."

"Suol right? That's what I heard…. right?"

"Yeah man."

"You got kids?"

"Yeah; a son and a daughter."

"What would you do if a nigga came into your crib and did the shit you did to my daughter?"

"Come on ma." He whined, damn near on the verge of tears.

"ANSWER THE FUCKIN' QUESTION!" D's voice boomed, but still got no answer. "Okay then." He said nodding head, heading back to his instruments. Turning back to him, he held a machete like weapon he twirled in his hand. "What arm did you use to hold my daughter?"

"Come on, I'll give you whatever you want."

"I want you to give me an answer to my question. What arm did you use to hold my daughter, messenger?"

"My…...my right?"

"That's what I thought." was D's response before swinging the machete, chopping his arm off. "Hold another baby now with your one-armed ass! You know what? I'm feeling generous because we killing so many birds with one stone tonight. Ain't that right Keon?"

"Fo' sho."

"So, I'm gonna give you a choice. Open or closed casket?"

Too busy screaming in pain, D made the choice for him; ending his life with a shot to the head. Removing a glove and then a blunt from his apron, D stood in front of Kyrie and fired up before he spoke.

"So you this niggas nephew huh? How?"

"I ain't telling you shit!" he hissed before spitting in his face. Taking Boz's cigarette from him, he put it out on his face. "How's that nigga your uncle?"

"He's my dad's brother, damn! Look, let me go now and maybe he'll take it easy on you."

"You funny. Ain't he funny?" D asked no one in particular. "How old are you?"

"21"

"21. You's a young buck huh? Who's your uncle?"

"You'll find out soon enough; nigga."

"I like this lil nigga right here. Too bad you related to the wrong mu'fucka." D said as he ribbed open his shirt before firing up a small blow torch. "Where your uncle at?"

"In your wife's pussy."

"Everybody got some shit to say about my wife. Although, she is a sexy mu'fucka. Ain't she a sexy mu'fucka?"

"Sure is. I don't know what she doing with your ass though."

"How you know she sexy?"

"Fuck you."

"Fuck me. Okay." D said putting a little flame to his nipple.

"Arghhhhh! Fuck!" Kyrie yelled.

"How you know my wife is sexy nigga?!"

"I saw pictures! Damn! Let me go!"

"Should we let him go?" D asked his crew.

"Hell naw!" Boz answered. "Even though that niggas nipple smell like bacon."

"What else can you tell me about my family?"

"I ain't got shit to say."

"You a tough lil nigga. Very admirable." He said putting the blow torch up to his other nipple.

"Okay! Okay!" he yelled before telling him all he knew; from the addresses of all their families and even that she'd just ordered baby furniture using her black card.

Knowing that they were thoroughly keeping tabs on his family, namely his wife, further pissed him off.

"You know what, the more I talk to you, the more you're pissing me off. So…. I'm gonna take it easy on you." He said cocking his 9. "Don't worry, you won't be lonely; the rest of your family is behind you." He gritted before poppin' him in the head. "Keep this nigga right here, I need to send a message. These other two niggas, get rid of they asses. Don't leave shit behind and Boz; get that fucking butt up. You aiight B? How's the chest?"

"I'm good. You aiight? Your ass might need a hug or some shit."

"I'm bought to go get that now."

Chapter 12

Having taken out damn near all of Rah's so called officers, they were no closer to finding out who he was or getting a lock on his location. It was like this nigga stayed in one place too long. As soon as they left New York, they headed to the address in Virginia. Not wanting to give away that they'd been there, they looked inside of the open windows to get a glimpse inside. They could see kids toys and not much furniture. The house barely looked lived in from what they could see. Just in case they were at the right address, D left a gift box on the front porch with the number to a burner phone inside.

Feeling a less human side of him threatening to take over, D retreated back to where he could always find peace and center himself; his wife and kids, the point of it all.

Opening the bedroom door, he could hear the shower running and Orchid singing from the bathroom. Stripping out of his clothes, he walked into the bathroom quietly and opened the shower door.

"Oh shit! You scared the hell outta me!" Orchid yelled, slapping his chest. When did you get here?" she asked, finally kissing his lips.

"Just a few minutes ago. You starting to like slapping a nigga a lil too much lately."

"Shut up, it was a reflex. I missed you."

"I missed you too. How you feeling? I see you starting to grow." He said, rubbing her small stomach.

"Yeah. I see you keeping me the way you said you wanted me; barefoot and pregnant."

"I can't help it that you got that bomb ass pussy and I wanting keep putting my babies in you. That's your fault."

"Oh yeah? Well maybe I need to be keeping my pussy to myself."

"Nah. You already got a nigga strung out like one of them niggas on The Corner. Daddy got a jones that needs to be satisfied." He said kissing on her neck. "Come here." He said, taking her hand as he sat on the seat in the shower.

Straddling his lap, Orchid slid down slowly on his hard dick that seemed to almost guide itself inside of her. Kissing him deeply, Orchid moved up and down slowly on his dick. Wanting to hit her bottom, D grabbed her hips, pulling her onto his length. Guiding her movements, she began a slow grind, feeling his dick hitting all the right spots.

"Damn ma this pussy wet as hell. Shit." D moaned as she rocked back and forth on him. "Fuck this shower shit." He said, standing with his dick still inside of her and her legs wrapped around his waist as he carefully carried her to the bed.

Laying her down, he put her legs up over her head and began lapping at her from her clit to her opening. Stiffening his tongue, he dipped it in and out of her hole, causing her to moan loudly. Spreading her legs, he settled between them and began sucking feverishly on her clit.

"This daddy's pussy?"

"Yes daddy! Shit yes!"

"Mmmm, this shit taste good as fuck." He moaned before lapping again at her clit before inserting his middle and index finger in her; pressing on her g-spot."

"Oh fuck! Shit daddy!"

"Yeah. Let daddy drink all your juices." He moaned as he began assaulting her clit again before putting his tongue back into her opening. Each time he brought his tongue out of her, it was coated with more and more of her cum. "Mmm. Hell yeah." He moaned, licking his lips and stroking his dick before playing in her juices before filling her up with a moan.

Wrapping her legs around him and pulling him close, O began to ride him from beneath. Biting his bottom lip sexily, the way she loved, he closed his eyes and began to moan; getting lost in the euphoric sensation that overcame his body as a result of her massaging his dick with her warm, tight pussy.

"Oh shit ma! Fuck!" he moaned, unable to hold back the nut he felt rising from his toes to his dick.

Grinding deep into her, their moans escalated as he dug deep inside of her. Playing with her clit, he quickened his strokes until her moans became screams of pleasure.

"Oh God. Daddy I love you so much!"

"I love you…. too. You love this…...dick?"

"Hell fucking…. yes, daddy. Uhhhhhh!" she moaned loudly as an orgasm too over her body.

Satisfied that she was satisfied, D stroked slow and deep until she came again and he was filling her up with his man milk. Sweaty and out of breath, he laid on her chest as she held him in her arms, running her hands across his wavy, fresh cut hair.

"Why can't it always be like this?" she asked softly, still gently rubbing his hair.

"We night go through our shit, but we always gonna come back to this ma. Matter of fact, as soon as all this bullshit is over and we get Kaliah back; I want to have that big wedding you used to talk about. You in a white dress looking like my queen. Well maybe not white, 'cause I done deflowered your ass repeatedly."

"You are such an ass." O perked and laughed. "Move."

"Where you going?"

"To go finish the shower I started before I was so rudely interrupted."

"You know you loved that shit." He said, reluctantly letting her up.

"Mmmm, damn right I did."

"Aiight, don't start shit back up. Fuck around and be hemmed up against that shower wall."

"Not if I lock this door." she teased, sticking her tongue out and making her ass bounce.

"Word?! You wouldn't."

Orchid winked her eye at him, slowly closing the bathroom door before slamming and locking it.

"Oh, she think shit's a game."

With her hands against the wall, head leaned forward as the water ran down her back, Orchid sang along with Jazmine Sullivan. Eyes closed and in her own world, she was pleasantly surprised by a hard dick pressing against her back. Turning and wiping the water out her eyes, she looked at D who stood wearing a smirk. Looking past him, she noticed part of the door broken off as a result of his break in.

"Now……. talk some more of that good shit."

Walking up to his front door with his daughter's hand in his, Rah leaned over to pick up the delivery that had been left on his porch. Opening the door for her to go inside, he checked the mailbox before closing the door behind him, setting the box on the table.

"Daddy can me order pizza for dinner? You can't cook that good."

"Word?! It's like that?" he couldn't do nothing but laugh. "Yeah, I'll order it now."

"I still love you though."

"I love you too." He said with a smile, pulling out his phone to place the order.

He'd done a lot of fucked up things in his life but the one good thing he did, helping create his beautiful daughter, overshadowed all that; at least that's the way he looked at it. After finishing the order, he flipped open his knife to open the box that he'd brought in. A foul odor hit his nose as he unraveled the plastic bag. Finally seeing what was inside of the box, his nostrils flared and his breathing quickened.

"Muthafucka!" he barked.

"You okay daddy?" his daughter asked, running into the foyer.

"Yeah, I'm good. Go 'head and finish watching tv, the pizza should be here soon."

"Okay." She perked, skipping bac off into the living room.

Pulling out his cell, he dialed Suol's number. He needed to know who had balls big enough to touch his blood. Getting no answer, he dialed Qua's number and got the same result. Finally noticing the note with the number attached, he grabbed his burner his used that disguised his voice and dialed the number.

"Hold on ma, I gotta take this." D said, putting a halt to her riding the hell out of his dick. "City morgue." He answered.

"You got jokes mu'fucka!" Rah spat into the phone.

"No more than you nigga. You thought your ass was untraceable huh? I found your bitch ass."

"Oh okay, this must be the infamous Damonte."

"The one and only pussy." He gritted. "Ma we gotta get back to this later." He said getting up. "You wanted my attention; now that you have it and I have yours, what the fuck you want?"

"Your fuckin' heart on a silver platter bitch. You touched my blood nigga. Until your ass is dead, everything you love is gonna disappear."

"And who's gonna help you with that? Your little messenger Suol? Your partner Qua? Your nephew the headless horse nigga sure can't help you. All them niggas done felt my wrath and your ass is next."

"I gotta give it to you; you got big balls for a lil ass nigga."

"Ask your moms, she'd be able to tell you."

"I'm gonna enjoy killing your disrespectful ass."

"In your wet dreams pussy. Who says I don't have my people outside your crib right now waiting to decapitate your ass like I did nephew? You talk a lot of shit for a nigga whose skirt has been pulled."

"I'mma see your ass soon."

"Make sure you wear your best prom dress bitch. I want you to look real pretty laid out in that casket." D spat and ended the call.

"D…. who was that?"

"That nigga Rah. Fuck boy ass nigga interrupting my nut."

"Did you ask if he knew anything about Kaliah?"

"I doubt that nigga got anything to do with it, but if he does, best believe I'mma find out. Don't worry, I'm gonna have lil mama back where she belongs without a scratch on her pretty lil head." He said kissing her forehead before throwing on some shorts and wife beater.

"Where you going?"

"To holla at Keon right quick. Why wsup?"

"You might wanna wash your dick first."

Chapter 13

"Hello." Mama T damn near sang into the phone.

"So, I hear you've been looking for me." The heavily accented voice said through the phone.

"Raul. It's been a long time. How have you been?"

"Dying, but I'm sure you knew that already. I don't want to have this conversation over the phone. Is it possible you and your children can fly out to my villa?"

"My children? Why do they need to be there?"

"Believe me, they'll want to be here to hear what I have to say. You'll hear from me in a couple of days." He said and ended the call.

"He's still an ignorant old bastard." She huffed as she dialed Orchid's number.

"Hey mom."

"Hey baby. Are you alone?"

"Yeah, D's out in the pool with the kids. Good; we need to talk."

Having lost track of Rah's slick ass, D and Keon were headed back to the states to flush this nigga out. As soon as Orchid kissed D's lips and closed the door, she began making calls. She knows from what he'd told her, that her credit cards and accounts were being tracked; so she needed to find a private pilot to fly her to and from Florida to meet with her mother.

Having finally secured a private plane, she packed a light bag and stopped to have the conversation she dreaded with Kiko.

"Where you think you going?" Kiko asked with her hand on her hip.

"I need to go to Florida to meet with mom."

"Why wouldn't she come here? She does know we're in the nigga protection program, right?"

"She does; which is why I hired a pilot plane to fly me there and back. I'm only making a pit stop in Miami; we're flying to Puerto Rico."

"Puerto…. Okay, what the fuck are you up to and why was my ass not included?"

"We're flying there to meet with Javier's brother."

"The dead brother?"

"Yeah; only he's not dead. Well, he's dying now. Anyway, he apparently has some information that'll help us figure out this whole Rah shit; but he won't tell her over the phone."

"Why you gotta carry your ass over there with her? O, this shit scares me. I don't think it's a good idea for you to go."

"He requested that me and B be there. I have to do this. Please just promise me, if anything happens……"

"Bitch, don't you even dare finish that sentence. You bring your big ass back here and in one fuckin' piece."

"Ko, you can't call D on this. If some shit goes wrong, then you tell him."

"I should call his ass so he can talk some sense…., better yet, tell your ass you can't go nowhere."

"I ain't feeling this shit either; but to put an end to this shit and have my family safe, I'm doin' this shit."

"I'd do the same boo. Call me to let me know you landed; and you better check in with me at least once a day or I will call D. Oh and when you're not on the plane, make sure you have your location on; it already saved your ass once."

"Yeah, tell me about."

"Alright then. You be safe, you carrying my nephew up in there." Ko said rubbing her stomach.

"Y'all getting' on my nerves with that shit there. I love you."

"I love you too. Tell my babies I love them too."

In flight on the way to Miami, Orchid was a bundle of nerves and had a good mind to have the pilot turn around. *"This is for my family."* she thought to herself as the plane began to land.

Hugging her brother, she got into the car headed towards her mother's house. Their flight would be leaving at three in the morning so they had a few hours to kill. As promised, she called Kiko to let her know she landed and to talk to Lil D. Ending her call, Orchid looked in her mother's direction, who seemed to be deep in thought.

"A penny for your thoughts."

"I'm just wondering what this is all about. All of the secrets I've kept hidden have all come out. This is some shit even I didn't know about; whatever it is."

"Well, at least we'll all be together when hear it."

"Orchid, do you know how to shoot a gun?"

"Mom, do you not know who I'm married to?"

"Okay; point taken. Raul may be dying but he's an evil old bastard with a lot of power over a lot of people; even in his condition. If the shit hits the fan, I wanna know I got back up."

"And since when did you learn how to shoot a gun?"

"You do know who *I* was married to?"

"Let me find out you're a gansta granny."

"Only in my spare time."

The pilot ride over was damn near silent, with very few words being exchanged between them. Orchid scrolled through pictures of her, D and the kids; praying that she'd make it back to them alive. She also had to say a separate prayer that she survived the wrath that was sure to come down on her when D finds out what she was up to.

Pulling up by way of limo to the massive estate, Orchid's mouth dropped open. The house was the most beautiful she'd ever seen. They came to a stop and one of the guards stationed outside their house opened the door.

"Mr. Vega is expecting you ma'am." He said, stone faced.

"Lead the way." Theresa said, falling in stride behind him.

Orchid and B were both blown away at how immaculate the house was. They were even more impressed by the inside. Once they were stopped in front of oversized double doors, they were led into a conference room. There were refreshments in the center of a round conference table and four chairs surrounding.

"Please have a seat and enjoy the refreshments. It takes Mr. Vega some time to get situated, so he'll be in momentarily."

"Thank you." Orchid said with a smile and a nod behind him. "Umm, isn't security supposed to pat you down for weapons on scan you or something?"

"Sis, it's something along those line; but you watch too many movies."

"Shut your ass up soccer dad." Orchid cracked.

"Alright you two. You're making me have a flash back of when you were younger."

"It's often like that with siblings. Even when you're older, you bicker with each other. Was the say way with my brother and I." Mr. Vega said as he entered the room on a motorized scooter, wearing oxygen. "Theresa, you're beautiful as always." He said holding a frail hand out towards her as he got closer.

"Thank you Raul. I'm sorry to hear about your condition."

"Shit. After four attempts on my life and a bout with prostate cancer, this is easy. Please, sit. So, these are your children? I haven't seen them since they were little bambinos. Orchid, you've grown into a beautiful young woman. Damonte is a lucky man."

"Thank you. Nice to meet you Mr. Vega."

"And Byron…...you look just like your father. The resemblance is uncanny."

"Thank you, it's nice to meet you."

"Please, enjoy a beverage or some fruit. Don't worry, everything is perfectly safe. I mean you no harm at all. So, I know you're wondering why I brought you all here."

"You would be right." Theresa said, anxious to know what exactly he knew."

"Bear with me, I'm an old man and the memory can get a little foggy. Anyway, you may not know it, but I loved your husband and father like my own brother. He, Roberto and myself made a lot of money together. Those were the good old days; when there was honor among thieves. Everything ran like a we; until oiled machine Roberto and Javier decided a two-way split was better than a four way split."

"I had no idea you were a part of things." Theresa said almost above a whisper.

"No one did; except for a select few. When Roberto brought to the table the idea of restructuring as he called it, Byron and I weren't happy about it at all. That's when the caca hit the fan. That was the second attempt on my life, which is when I went into hiding. You see, y brothers were, stupid ignorant fucks. We were supposed to meet up, as we normally did every month to go over the books. I got there and Byron hadn't shown up yet. My brother's and I got to arguing and they revealed their hand. My own flesh and blood shot me multiple times."

"Hold up. The whole reason Javier was supposed to have killed my dad was because he killed you and Roberto." B gritted.

"Yes, that was his justification to kill your dad. Your father is actually responsible for me making it out of there alive and set up I hiding. Roberto was set up by Javier so he could control the family on his own. I hurt me immeasurably when your father was killed. I had no doubt that Javier was responsible."

"If you knew Javier killed him, why didn't you do anything?" Orchid asked with tears in her eyes.

"Oh meha. Although it was easy for my own brothers to try to take my like, I couldn't take Javier's. He had a young daughter and was left to raise Roberto's two children. With me being 'dead', I couldn't very well take them and I couldn't leave them to fend for themselves; they were way too young."

"So my husband was killed for nothing?"

"Unfortunately so Theresa. After my dear friend was killed, Javier felt a difference in his pockets. You see, Byron controlled most of the tristate area. Everyone loved and respected him. They also suspected foul play in regards to his death and didn't want to do business with Javier. With his business dwindling and have difficulty moving product, he decided to link up with a younger, new breed. That's where Damonte and Keon came in. They came in and put him back where he needed to be financially. They were making money hand over fist; which is why he let them run things as they saw fit. Each and every month he got his money, no problem. Once Damonte and Keon decided to retire and settle down, not that I blame him…." He said and paused with a wink. "His cash cow was no more. Grasping at straws he linked up with two more partners."

"Okay, so who are these partners?" Byron asked.

"One of his former partners I'm sure you've indirectly already encountered. Before we get to him, it's the other partner you need be most concerned with. Theresa, I'm so sorry to have to be the one to tell you this but; Byron has another son."

"He what?!" she and Byron yelled in unison.

"Unfortunately this is true. During his stays in New York, he met a Spanish woman; Marta. She was a waitress at a club we used to frequent whenever we were in town. At first it was innocent, subtle flirting; before long, she was openly flirting with him. After a couple of months, she became a fixture in his life. Whenever we were in town, she'd be around. A few months after they began dating, she began to pressure him about leaving you and making her his wife. At that point, Byron ended things with her; but not before she became pregnant."

"That bastard! If he were alive right now, I'd kill his ass!" Theresa huffed.

"I believe you would." He said patting her hand. "When she told him she'd gotten pregnant, he insisted she get rid of the baby. Against his wishes, she kept the baby;

taking his money and tell him she'd gotten the baby aborted."

"Damn, I guess that really is the oldest trick in the book." Byron huffed, shaking his head at having been got the same way.

"That it is. Anyway, she gave birth to a son; Antonio Perez."

"So, where is he now; and did he know about dad?" Orchid asked.

"Not only did he know about your dad; over the years he'd been keeping tabs on you all; watching you from afar."

"Why not make contact; introduce himself?"

"Thanks to his venom spewing mother, he developed a hatred for your dad; and all of you. You and everyone you love are in danger."

Chapter 14

For over a week, D was obsessed with trying to track down Rah. He also found it odd that no one at all knew a thing about Kaliah's disappearance. Every time he went back home and he had to tell Orchid he had no leads on her location, it broke his heart a little more.

Before they left New York, Keon decided to stop past his cousin Danita's house to holla at one of his favorite cousins and see is she'd seen Khalil at all. Before he could even knock on the door, she was snatching the door open and jumping into his arms.

"Damn girl! You gonna warn a nigga before you throw all that on him. You know you got a big ass."

"Kiss my big ass. It's so good to see you. What brings you around?"

"I was in the area. Wanted to come holla at you before I left. I like what you did with the place." Keon said, walking around taking in the décor of the brownstone he'd help her purchase."

"Thank you. I'm trying to be like you a lil somethin' when I grow up." She cracked. "You rude as hell. Who's your fine ass friend?"

"You need to calm your nasty ass down. He's taken and trust, you don't want no static with his other half. D, this my crazy ass cousin Danita. Danita, my brother from another mother D."

"Nice to meet you Danita." D said with a smile, reaching out a hand for her to shake.

"Damn! We practically family and no hug? You must have one of those clothes sniffing, pocket checking wives huh?"

"Not at all. I ain't going nowhere and I don't do shit to make her think it's necessary for her to do all of that."

"Well, you tell her I said she's a lucky ass woman. If you change your mind though, you know where to find me. Unh!"

"You need to calm your hot ass down. What you got up in here to eat? A nigga hungry and I smell food."

"You always hungry and smell food."

"Quit holding out. What you got?" D asked, the smell of the food making his mouth water.

"Some fried catfish, baked mac and cheese with a little cabbage.

"Damn! I came on the right day. I'm gonna need some of that mac and cheese to go. Yo D, she makes some of the best mac and cheese."

"We'll see about that."

"A shit talker, I like that. Let me make y'all asses a plate before your big ass starts diggin' in my shit."

"If you know what's good for you, you'll handle that."

After having two plates and smoking a blunt with his cousin, it was time for them to head to the air strip. Orchid hadn't been answering her phone and Kiko was acting real strange about something, so he needed to look her in the eye and pick her brain. Getting up from his seat to hug Danita, the kitchen door swung open.

"Aunt Nita, I'm…... Daddy D!" Kaliah perked running to D, jumping into his arms. "Did you come to pick me up?"

"Baby girl!" D said holding her tight. "Yes I did. Me and your mom have been looking all over for you."

"Daddy D? Okay, what the hell is going on."

"This is his step daughter. D is married to Orchid."

"That's your wife?! That's my girl; well, we only chilled a couple of times. Khalil said he had custody of Kaliah now."

"The nigga took her over a month ago. He was supposed to have her for a week and never brought her back. Changed his number, the whole shit." Keon gritted.

"I missed you too Uncle Keon." Kaliah said hugging him.

"I missed you lil mama."

"Kaliah, go grab your stuff, we're going home. Mommy has been wanting to see you."

"I'm supposed to keep her until he comes back."

"When is that?" D asked.

"In two days. He said he had business out of town."

"Tell that nigga your services weren't needed. Tell him I said it and he can holla at me." Keon said, pissed.

"Hey, I don't want no static. If he took her from her mother, by all means; take her."

"I'm ready!" Kaliah perked, running back into the kitchen.

"Give Nita a hug and say thank you." D said, smiling at her. He couldn't wait to walk into the house with her and saw Orchid's face.

"Thank you Aunt Nita. Tell daddy I'll see him later and to keep taking cooking lessons for when I come back."

"She is definitely her mother's child." Keon cracked.

D scooped her up, planting kisses on her face headed towards the door while Keon chopped it up with his cousin. Securing her in a seat belt, he smiled and listened attentively while she told him all about the time she'd spent with her dad. He wore a smile on her face as she talked but he was distracted from the conversation by thoughts of killing Khalil.

"Oh shit!" Lil D perked, running to his sister when they walked through the door. Grabbing onto her tight, he picked her up and spun her around. "You're a pain in my butt, but I missed you."

"I missed you too. Does that mean I can play your video game now?"

"Don't push it."

"What did you say lil boy?" D asked, looking at him trying to hold back laughter.

"I mean…. oh shot. My bad dad."

"I'll give you a pass this time."

"Boy, what you in here making all that noise for? You know those kids are sleep." Kiko said walking into the living room. "Oh shit! My Lia!" she perked, picking her up. "I'm so happy to see you."

"I'm happy to see you too. Where's Keona and KJ?"

"Upstairs napping. They should be up soon. Go 'head and play with your brother so I can talk to your dad and uncle."

"Okay!"

"Where's ma, out shopping?" D asked, anxious for her to see Kaliah.

"Not exactly." she mumbled. *"Damn why these niggas back so soon?"* she thought.

"Not exactly? What's that mean? Where she at?" Keon asked, wasting no time going. One thing he knew and loved about his wife, she couldn't look him in the face and lie.

"You guys must be hungry. You want some dinner?" she asked, attempting to turn and leave the room.

"Unh uh. Don't even." Keon said, grabbing her arm.

"Where she at sis?" D asked, knowing he was about to hear something that pissed her off.

"She's in Puerto Rico with mom and B. Shit!"

"Puerto Rico?!" D and Keon yelled.

"What the fuck she doing there?" D asked, chewing the inside of his cheek.

"You might want to talk to her about that."

"I would; except her ass ain't answering her phone! I need to know what the fuck is going on and where she's at. It's not safe for her out here."

"I don't know exactly where they are. She said her mom got in touch with dude's supposedly dead brother. He had some shit to reveal to them but wanted them to fly out to meet him. That's all I know, she hasn't called yet today."

"What?! How long she been gone?" D gritted.

"A little over a day."

"Muthafucka!" D boomed. "She got her location on?"

"She should. I told her to make sure she kept it on."

"When her ass calls, I don't give a shit what she says; come get me."

Heading up the stairs, D was a combination of worried and pissed. *"I knew her ass was gonna pull some shit like this!"* he thought to himself as he dialed her number. Getting her voicemail only further infuriated him and had him about ready to hope a plane to Puerto Rico; even with him not knowing exactly where she was.

"Now you know you shouldn't have let her ass leave." Keon said looking at her with scolding eyes before shaking his head and walking away.

"What did you expect me to do? You know how her ass is when she makes her mind up about something."

"Your ass could've called. Y'all a trip. Let me go check on this nigga. Her ass call, don't let her off the phone until he talks to her."

Kiko had given the kids dinner, baths and put them to bed and Orchid still hadn't called. Not only that, Keon and D hadn't said much of anything to her except for to ask if Orchid had called. *"I'm gonna kick her ass when she gets her ass back here for putting me in the middle of this shit!"* she said to herself. Her thoughts were interrupted by her cell ringing in her pocket.

"You bitch!" Kiko answered, seeing it was Orchid.

"What I do to your ass?"

"Heffa your husband is here and he is pissed! Now their asses are pissed off at me because I let you leave and didn't call."

"Damn! I was hoping to be back before he got there. Are the kids okay?"

"They're fine…...even Kaliah."

"Kaliah? How do you know?"

"When your husband walked in he had her with him."

"Oh thank God!" she perked, her voice cracking from emotion. "Where is she?"

"They're all upstairs sleep. After she talked us to death, ate and got a bath; that ass was out."

"Oh god I can't wait to hug and kiss all over her."

"When your ass coming back?"

"We're leaving tomorrow and I'll be back to the house."

"You better be. Hold on, your husband wants to talk to you."

"Shit."

"Shit is right." Kiko said handing D the phone, leaving back out the bedroom to continue the laundry.

Turning on the washer, Kiko began to check the pockets of the kid's clothes before putting them into the washer. Looking down, she noticed Kaliah's backpack. Picking it up, she unzipped it and shook the contents out on the top of the dryer. Shaking out a pair of her shorts, something fell out of the pocket; pinging against the metal.

"KEON! KEON, GET IN HERE NOW!" she yelled at the top of her lungs, not wanting to touch whatever it was.

"What you yellin' for? Oh, you trying to get it in again on the washing machine?"

"No you pervert. What is that?"

"What's what?"

"That little thing there that looks like a chip."

Leaning into get a closer look, Keon's face dropped. "Go upstairs and tell D to come down here." he said pulling out his phone to take a picture and send off in a text. "Pack a couple of things for you and the kids and get them dressed."

"Keon, they're sleeping."

"Ma, we don't have time for this shit! Do it!" he barked, pissed off that he may be right about what the 'chip' could be.

Receiving a text back from Boz, he confirmed exactly what he thought it was. Khalil's bitch ass planted a tracking device in Kaliah's bag.

"What up nigga?" D asked, walking into the laundry room.

"This is what's up?" he said handing him the device. The dark look in his eyes let him know that he realized what it was he was holding.

"This muthafucka! We need to get them outta here now."

"Ma upstairs packing and getting the kids together now. You wanna smash that shit or what?"

"Nah. He wanted to know where we were, let him find out. When his ass walk up in this bitch, I'mma light that ass up. You sure we......"

"We don't even need to discuss that; I already done told you."

"Aiight then. It's on."

Chapter 15

With Raul becoming easily exerted, he had his staff get Theresa, Orchid and B set up in his guest house to freshen up and have dinner while he rested. Knowing that D was back and had Kaliah with him, made Orchid more anxious to get back. Wanting to be respectful, she had to bid her time until he was ready to continue.

"I still can't believe Pop's went and had a son. This shit is crazy." B said, shaking his head.

"I had a feeling he was involved with someone, but never did I think it had gotten so serious. Another child? I wish he was still alive so I could beat his ass." Theresa fussed.

"Well, there's nothing we can do about it now; and reaching out isn't an option, since he apparently hates us." Orchid added. "I'm still a little lost though; and what about this conversation could he not tell us over the phone?"

"For real." B co-signed.

"Well, we don't know what else it is that he has to tell is. So, let's wait and see. Please tell me one of you has a blunt."

"Let me find out you a full blown pot head now mom." Byron cracked.

"You're not too old to get your ass whipped."

KNOCK! KNOCK! KNOCK!

"Mr. Vega requests you join him back in the conference room please." One of his housemen announced.

"I guess I'll take a raincheck on that blunt." Theresa said leading the way.

"Please excuse me. I can't do too much before this old body of mines tells me it needs a rest. Did you enjoy your dinner? Where the guest quarters suitable for you?"

"Everything was great. Thank you Mr. Vega. I'm gonna need the recipe for that pork." Orchid said with a smile.

"I'll have Magda give you her recipe. Now, where were we. Yes, Antonio. He became obsessed with your family and because his mother repeatedly telling him so, he felt like your father abandoned him because he wasn't good enough. He was the bastard child that didn't fit into his perfect family. Marta also had another child by an associate of ours; thinking it would make Byron jealous. With the assistance of that associate, her second child's father; they became the competition of your husband and his partner, although they had no idea. They ran the areas of New York that Damonte and Keon didn't control and parts of the Midwest; until they began to lose territory. Then they began harboring ill will. So when they were approached by Javier to partner up to take out their mutual completion, they jumped the opportunity."

"The enemy of my enemy is my friend." B added.

"Exactly. Now that Javier is dead, Antonio holds all the cards. While he is the slower of the two to anger, he's also most evil. Trust me when I say, he will not stop until he gets what he wants; and that's revenge on those he feels kept him away from having a relationship with his father."

"Do you have a picture of him?" Theresa asked.

"This picture was taken three months ago of him in New York."

"Oh my God. That's D he's sitting right behind." Orchid gasped.

"Yes. I've been having my people follow him; running interference where I can. Sad to say, when I'm gone, there's not much else I can do to help."

"I've seen him. He was at my wedding!"

"That's what he does. Sneaky little bastard. Until I take my last breath, I and my associates will do what I can to help protect you. Orchid my dear, I'm sorry to tell you that you and your family are in the most imminent danger; even hiding in Turks and Caicos, your location has been found out. His brother and the few men he does have left are on their way there now."

"What?!" Orchid yelled, rising from her seat. "How did they know? How did you know?"

"As I've said, I loved your father like my brother and I promised I would look out for his family if anything ever happened to him."

"We have to go. I have to get to my family."

"Calm yourself my dear; well, as much as you can given the current situation. I have some of my men there to protect your family. Not even Damonte and Keon are aware of their presence. Please have a seat. You need to hear the rest of what I have to say."

"It's gonna be okay sis." Byron said taking her hand.

"I'm sorry to say beautiful Orchid, you were a pawn in their revenge plot."

"Come again."

"It was meant for Antonio's brother to get close to you, earn your trust, rob you blind and then kill you; all to hurt Damonte and to satisfy Antonio's blood lust. What they didn't factor in was that Javier was a bigger snake than they. With Damonte "dead" there was no need in making him suffer."

"So they didn't know that Javier had D alive and working for him?"

"Exactly. Another thing they didn't plan on was Antonio's brother falling in love with you."

"Okay, I'm not quite sure what you're trying to tell me."

"Antonio's brother's name is Eduardo Khalil Perez."

"D......did you just say Khalil?" Orchid asked, her voice shaking and tears streaming down her face.

"Unfortunately it is true my dear. They've had this plan in the making for some time. If you recall, Khalil's father and Keon's mother were to marry at one point. So this has been a slow, deliberate, poorly executed plan."

"I can't......I can't believe this is happening to me."

"I'm sorry to have to deliver this news to you my dear, but I could no longer keep these things in. With Khalil having a vulnerable spot, which is you and Kaliah, Antonio is planning something in case he fails again. What that is, I have no idea; but as soon as I get the information, you will have it also. Again, I am so sorry."

"It's not your fault Raul. I appreciate more than you could ever know, you sharing this information with us."

"I felt it was my duty to do so. If there is anything else I can do to assist, just ask it and it's yours. Theresa, you know how to contact me."

"I do."

"Oh God! I have to warn D and Keon!"

"Do what you must. As soon as you are ready my car will take you back to the airstrip and fly you wherever you need to go."

"Mr. Vega, thank you." Orchid said softly before kissing his cheek.

"Damonte is a very lucky man; and you two are lucky to have such a strong, beautiful woman as your mother."

"Such a flatterer you are."

"It's nice to meet you again Mr. Vega. Thank you, for everything you've done for my family; and having my pops back."

"Of course, it was my pleasure. I'd do it all again."

"Byron, take your sister outside to the car; I'll be right behind you."

"I got her." Byron said, putting his arm around Orchid leading her out to the car.

"Thank you."

"You don't have to keep thanking me. I love you all like my family. Had things turned out differently, they may have been my children."

"I hope to see you again. Take care of yourself." Said lightly kissing his lips. "It's been too long."

"Way too long. Go ahead. Don't kept them waiting." He said reluctantly letting go over her hand, watching her walk through the door. "Theresa?"

"Call if you need anything."

"I will."

Kissing his kids and Kiko on the cheek, D watched as Keon drove off with them in route to a location where they would be safe until shit blew over. Not knowing who, what or when to expect it, D armed the alarm system and headed to the basement where they kept an arsenal of weapons. After arming himself to the tee, he went throughout the house stashing weapons; so if needed, he'd have one in arm's length. While stashing a gun under the couch the alarm began to blare. Unable to see clearly to the front door, he scaled the wall approaching slowly, both guns drawn. Ready to fire, the foyer light came on; stopping him just before he squeezed the trigger.

"Nigga! You were supposed to call when you were on the way back. You lucky your big ass turned on that light. I don't know how the fuck I'd explain that shit to Kiko. It was an accident wasn't gonna cut it."

"If you shot me you wouldn't have to worry about just her. I would've haunted the shit outta your ass."

"You ready for this shit?"

"Nigga, you act like it's world war three. It's just Khalil and his band of merry fuck boys."

"I don't know nigga. Some shit ain't sitting right with me. Strap up my nigga, I think it's about to be some shit."

Chapter 16

A bundle of nerves, Orchid repeatedly tried to call D on the way to the air strip. When she couldn't get an answer from him, she tried Kiko and Keon and got the same result. All she could do was pray and hope that here family were all alive and safe.

With a half hour left to kill before they would be ready to take off, Orchid shook nervously. Sitting down next to her Byron placed a hand on her leg to still it, lit a blunt and passed it to her.

"Where you get that from?" she asked, taking the fatty before he could answer.

"Mr. Vega's houseman. He heard us talking and had a whole cigar box of these shit rolled up in the car. I'm surprised your bloodhound ass ain't sniff it out. It's some official too"

"I see." She said attempting to hold in the thick smoke before coughing violently.

"Damn girl; go easy. I just told you this was some official."

"I got this! I was just caught off guard. Gimmie that." She said taking the L and pulling on it again. "I can't believe this shit."

"What? That pops had another kid?"

"That too; but the fact that I was sleeping with the enemy. I love my daughter and have no regrets at all but damn!"

"I can't even imagine how you must be feeling."

"Played, hurt, betrayed. Even if the original plan was just to get close to me, why father my child. Had it not been for D 'coming bac from the dead', I would've married this nigga. Who know what he could have done to me, my son; shit, all of you. This shit is just too much."

"It's easier said than done, but calm down O. We're gonna get to the house and put an end to all of this shit."

"Even if it ends with Khalil, what about our dear brother?"

"I guess we'll cross that bridge when we get to it; but we'll do it together. Aiight?" B asked, putting his arm around his sister; pulling her close.

"Well damn!" Theresa perked, having opened the car door and smoke greeting her. Y'all couldn't wait for me?"

"Sorry mom. I needed this."

"We also need these." She said, dropping a small duffle bag that contained guns and ammo.

"What the fuck?! First an unknown brother, then my almost brother in law is a snake and now I find out my mom is Dirty Harriet. There ought to be a daily limit on bullshit intake."

"Boy, shut your ass up. After this is over, I better not hear about your ass picking up another gun. I can't lose you again; I can't lose either of you but this is for the family. You got me?"

"Yeah mom."

"Excuse me?"

"Yes mom, I got you."

"That's better. You, I don't have to worry about; y poor urbanely challenged baby. I should've let you out more."

"Really?! I'm emotionally distraught over here and you got jokes?"

"I'm sorry baby. Just trying to make light of the situation. If it comes down to it, killing a person isn't too bad. It's kind of a stress reliever."

"Okay, I'm gonna need for this day to be over. This is too damn much right now."

Before boarding the plane, Orchid tried D a couple more times and still got no answer. Dialing Kiko and finally getting an answer, Orchid cried tears of joy.

"Oh thank God! Are you guys okay?! Y'all have to get out of the house."

"We're fine and we're already out of the house. Where are you? Are you okay?"

"I'm fine, considering. We're on our way back to the house."

"O.…...go.……. house."

"I can't hear you, say it again." She said louder into the phone. "Hello?! Shit!"

"What did she say? Are she and the kids okay?"

"She said they were out of the house. I think she was telling me to go to the house."

"To the house it is."

Sitting in a dark living room playing Madden and sharing a blunt, D was beginning to think the whole tracking incident was bullshit. Just as he was about to score a touchdown on Keon, the motion sensor alerted before the power went out.

"Looks like it's on my nigga." Keon said softly, cocking his guns.

"True that. Stay alive my nigga."

"You do the same."

Moving quickly through the dark living room, they crouched next to the stair case; outta sight waiting for the first move to be made. The front door was kicked open and a dark figure stood in the doorway. As he began moving through the foyer, two more figures appeared behind him; guns drawn, moving behind him towards the living room.

"Check upstairs." The head nigga said above a whisper.

As soon as they heard his feet hit the stairs, they both lit into him from beneath. Moving quickly, they got out of dodge before the bullets began to rip through the hidden closet they'd just occupied. Coming from around the corner D opened fire on the two niggas that stood in the living room.

The patio door came crashing in a more niggas came through the kitchen, into the hallway. Keon turned and opened fire, watching the bodies fall to the floor.

"D! Down!" Keon yelled, seeing a red beam on his back.

Following the beam outside of the living room window, Keon opened fire; taking out the window and the person that attempted to take out D.

"Good looking my nigga." D huffed at the close call.

"I got you my nigga."

"Check this shit out." D said above a whisper as he noticed two cars full of niggas pull up and approach the house. "Damn, I thought we killed most of his niggas."

"He must've went on www.fuckboyondemand.com and ordered up some more. We need to move upstairs. Down here looks like Swiss cheese."

Climbing the stairs quietly, they each took a bedroom in the master suite. Pulling out the AK's he had stashed under the bed, he handed Keon one, eased back the drape and took aim.

D smiled wickedly as he licked off shots into the driveway. Dust from the bullets hitting the water fountain out front impaired the vision of the men hiding behind it; making it easy for them to hit their targets. Not seeing any more bodies moving, D took the time to reload his weapon.

"Let's split up and check room by room. D whispered.

"Let's do this."

Chapter 17

Orchid's legs couldn't carry her to her car fast enough when their plane landed. Jumping in and starting the motor, she sped up to the curb where she had her mom wait for her to get in.

Due to them having unregistered weapons in the car, she had to obey all traffic rules so not to get pulled over. Calling D's phone repeatedly, she still got no answer.

"Shit!" she huffed.

"I'm sure he's fine sis. We'll be there soon."

Barely able to contain herself during the drive, she had to pull over and let B finish the drive to the house.

As they approached the area were they're temporary home was, B stopped on the side of the road. Checking to make sure all of the guns were locked and loaded, B handed two to each of them before continuing towards the house. Stopping a little way down the road, Byron turned off the lights and killed the engine.

"I'm gonna get out first and go around the back. O, wait until I send you a text before you come out. Mom, you stay here and don't come out unless it's an absolute emergency."

"Boy, I can handle myself."

"Just stay. Text if you see or hear anything." B said before couching low, taking off towards the house.

"I'm not just gonna sit here and do nothing. My husband could be dead in there. I'm not gonna lose him again."

"Orchid, please just wait for your brother."

"Mom, I'll be fine. Wait here." Orchid said getting out the car.

Crouching down as she'd seen her brother do, she headed towards the front door of the house. Covering her mouth to keep from screaming, she looked around at all the bodies scattered around the lawn. Looking back up at the house and seeing all the bullet holes, she took off running inside.

Gun in her shaking hand, Orchid crept slowly through the front door. Looking around the he foyer and living room, all she saw was death. Hearing glass crack behind her, she turned around with her gun raised.

"Damn! You're more beautiful than the last time I saw you ma. How you been?"

"How do you think I've been Khalil? Or do you prefer King Rah?"

"Ha.......I guess you got me figured out huh? How did you know?"

"It helps to know people in high places; you asshole."

"Is that any way to talk to the man you almost married and the father of your child?"

"How would you have me talk to you? You used me!"

"You got it all wrong; well some of it. Yeah, I was supposed to find you, get close to you and kill you initially; but when I laid eyes on you, I fell in love. Before I could fight it, your sexy ass had me wrapped around your finger."

"How did your brother feel about that?"

"Damn! You really have done your research. I'm proud of you girl!" he perked. "Our brother was pissed the fuck off; still is. He seriously has a hard on for you and your family; but my family was more important. Well the family I almost had. Shit would've been so much easier had your fuckin' husband stayed dead. Why Orchid?"

"Why what?"

"Why did you choose him over me?"

"I didn't choose him; he chose me. Some loves can never die. Even when he was 'dead' I felt him and didn't want to let go; until I met you. I thought that you were my second chance at true love but the universe has a way of paying cruel jokes on you. It's a good thing that did happen. What were you gonna do once we were married huh? Kill me and my family; the run away with Kaliah?"

"At first; well yeah. You don't understand how much I love you. I went against my blood for you and our daughter! Then you let this punk ass nigga come in and fuck everything up! You thought I was good with that shit?! Fuck no! So, here's what we gonna do; we're gonna make a choice. When I say we, I mean you and your dear old husband. Bring your ass out here nigga!" Khalil yelled out into the house and got no response. "You taking too long nigga! As much as I love her ass, I will put a bullet in her fuckin head!"

"You don't need to do all that." D said coming from the back of the house. "Let her go, this is between me and you."

"You're in no fuckin' position to make any demands nigga. This is between all of us. Tell your boy to bring his ass out here….and Byron's punk ass. Bring your ass niggas!"

"This is how we do shit now nigga?" Keon gritted.

"Keon, you my man a hundred grand and all; you just aligned yourself with the wrong nigga. So, now that the gang is all back together, we gonna do it like this. Orchid, you can save yourself by choosing to get our daughter and coming with me. Or and the lil bastard you're carryin' can die right along with them. Make your choice."

"O, I love you more than myself. You're the best thing that's ever happened to me. I can't have you lose your life because of me. If I've never did anything right in life, the one thing I did right was making you my wife. Just make sure that our kids know that I love them very much."

"Yeah, yeah, yeah! All this shit is real touching but I got moves to make. So what's it gonna be?"

"Get the fuck away from my daughter!" Theresa said firing a shot, hitting Khalil in the shoulder.

"Fuck! Mom's packin'?!" he said ducking for cover. "Send them nigga in. Kill everybody in this bitch." He yelled into his phone.

"Take Orchid and go Mom!" D shouted pushing them out the way.

Ducking and running through the back of the house, bullets whizzed past their heads.

"Who the fuck are you?" D asked the Spanish man that had his back to his busting off shots.

"Mr. Vega sent us to help." He yelled over the gun fire.

Theresa and Orchid laid on the ground as gunfire erupted through the house. When it all came to a halt, Orchid jumped up and ran into to house yelling for D.

"Damonte! Keon! B! Where are you?" she yelled, frantically looking around what used to be the downstairs area of their house."

"Sis! Over here!" Byron yelled.

"Shit! You're hit."

"Just in the leg, I'm straight." He gritted as she helped him up. "Keon! Yo Keon!"

"I'm good." He said rolling a body that partially covered him, off. "D…. you good my nigga? D!"

"D! Baby answer me."

"Fuck! O, over here."

"NO! No, no, no! Baby please. Don't do this to me." Orchid cried, slapping his face until he opened his eyes.

"You know......I hate....it when you.... cry." he strained to get out.

"Don't try to talk baby, we're gonna get you some help. Keon, please!"

"I'm on it. Hang in there my nigga." He said running out the house to grab the truck.

"O.... I meant what I said. You're.... you my angel. I love you." He said attempting to close his eyes."

Slapping him hard across his face, his eyes popped back open. "Damn. I'm shot and you......still hitting on a......nigga."

"I'm sorry......"

"I'm sorry you keep choosing this nigga over me." Khalil said with a gun to her neck. "Get your ass up. NOW!"

"Khalil, you don't have to do this." she said as tears slid down her face; inching her hand into her jeans for her Tiffany gun

"You think this shit is a fuckin' game huh?! Turn your ass and look at me. I don't like shooting niggas in the back."

"Khalil......"

"What bitch?!"

POW! "I'll always choose D!" she yelled as she watched his body drop to the floor.

Kicking his gun away from his reach, she dropped to her knees, pacing D's head into her lap.

"Let me find......out you ......bodying niggas for ya......man."

"I heard a shot! What was that?!" Keon ran through the front door with his gun drawn.

"I handled it."

"You…...you handled what?!"

Nodding her head towards Khalil, Keon walked over to his body. Letting another shot off in his chest, he rushed back over to D; scooping him up to carry him out to the waiting truck.

Hopping into the back seat, Orchid laid D's head in her lap; talking to him to make sure he stayed awake until they could get him some medical attention. *"Lord, I humbly approach you in prayer to ask that you spare my husband's life. Although we are all imperfect and have sinned numerous times, I pray for forgiveness for both him and myself. I also pray that you bless and keep my entire family safe from evil and harm. I pray these things in the name of son Jesus Christ. Amen"*

Chapter 18

Nine months later......

Theresa held onto three-month old baby Dionte, who donned a white Armani tux, while the stylist put the finishing touches on Orchid's hair. When she was finished, she passed him off to the Nanny while she helped Orchid into her Vera Wang mermaid dress with lace bodice. Taking the diamond tiara from its case, Theresa crowned her daughter before adding her veil.

"Wow." Theresa said emotionally. "I thought you were the most beautiful bride I'd ever seen the first time you got married. You've topped yourself honey. You look amazing."

"Aww. Thank you mom."

"I almost forgot. Your husband sent up a little something new for you to wear."

Pulling a chocolate and white diamond choker from the velvet box, she placed it around her neck; along with a matching bracelet.

"Bling Bling bitch!" Kiko perked.

"Ohhhh, Aunt Kiko said a bad word!" Kaliah perked.

"Auntie's sorry. We better get going, your militant ass wedding planner says we have ten minutes to get in place."

"We better go, because she has one more time and I'm gonna snatch that yaki made wig right off her head." Theresa huffed.

"She don't want those problems." Orchid cracked. "Let's go, my fine ass husband is waiting for me at altar."

"You ready for this bruh?" Keon asked, nudging D.

"Watch that shit nigga. You know I'm still the designated handicap." He cracked. As a result of his gunshot wounds, he had to walk with the assistance of a cane. "You act like we ain't already married."

"My wedding gift to y'all is a year's supply of condoms. Y'all niggas keep fucking like y'all do, you gonna end up with a Brady Bunch."

"That's what I want nigga. Fuck a condom." He said in a whisper with the preacher now standing next to them.

The music began and the doors opened. Lil D, their ring bearer, came down the aisle holding the pillow with the rings in one hand while pulling baby Dionte in a custom wagon. Kiko came down the aisle looking flawless in a champagne colored, roman inspired dress that hugged her curves just right.

"Sis don't look half bad; with her ugly ass." D cracked.

"Fuck you; my wife is beautiful nigga."

"I guess you're right."

"THE BRIDE IS COMING! THE BRIDE IS COMING!" Kaliah and Keona yelled, coming towards them tossing down rose petals.

The wedding march played and the double doors opened. Not one to show too much emotion, the vision before him made his breathing stop and a lump form in his throat. Before he could stop it, tears flowed down his cheeks as his beautiful wife approached; escorted by her brother. Clapping Bryon up and pulling him into a brotherly hug, he turned to look at the vision of beauty before him; who also had tears staining her face.

Taking her hand to help her up the stairs, he couldn't help but to lift her veil and kiss her before they got started. They're guests whistled and applauded as he tongued her down in from of man, God and everyone else.

"If you're done, we can get started." their officiator cracked. "Dearly beloved, we are gathered here today in from of friends, family and God to renew the vows of this man and woman. The couple has written their own vows. Orchid, the floor is yours."

"Damonte, I never would have guess the day I met you that my life would truly began. Although I played hard to get, I eventually gave in to your thuggish charm; and it was the best decision I've made in my life. As all couples do we've had our ups and downs, but our love sustains up; not even death can keep us apart. The day we first proclaimed our love for each other and took those vows, I married the yen to my yang. I love you with my whole heart and soul; 'til death do us part." she finished with a smile and tears in her eyes.

"Damn! How do I top that? Orchid, the day I met you, I truly found my rib. I knew on that day, that I'd found the mother of my children, the love of my life and my best friend. You ma, are the air I breathe. Without you, there is no me. I thank you for being the best friend, mother and lover a man could ever ask for. Beside the occasional, unintentional screw up; I plan on spending the rest of my life doing whatever it takes to keep you happy. I love you with every fiber of my being; 'til death do us part."

"After that, I don't think there's anything else that needs to be said. The rings please." After a brief prayer over the rings and their union, he states, "I'd like to present to you again, Mr. and Mrs. Damonte Dewitt Sr. You may kiss your bride......again."

D bopped coolly down the aisle with his cane as they left out of the church, headed to their limo. Holding her hand and looking into her eyes, D had to thank God for sending him an angel by the damn of Orchid.

"Don't even think about it."

"Think about what? I was just thinking about how beautiful you are and how lucky I am to have you as my wife."

"And?"

"And how if you didn't have on all that dress I'd have you riding this big dick right now. Damn!"

"That's what I knew; nasty ass."

Walking into the reception area to applause, they headed straight to the middle of the dancefloor for their second first dance. D threw his cane to Keon and pulled his wife close as Anthony Hamilton crooned 'The Point of It All'. Grabbing her ass and kissing her through most of the song, D's dick was rock hard by the time the song ended.

"You gonna have to keep that under wraps until later daddy."

"Come on ma, let's dip off into one of these closets or something."

"I don't think so. You'll have to wait 'til later. Don't worry, I have a lil something special in store for you later."

"I like the way that shit sounds. Unh!" he groaned, slapping her on her ass.

"Get that cane from Keon and stop showing off. I'm going up to the room to change."

"Hurry up. You know I ain't trying to be socializing with all these niggas too long; that's your thing."

"Stop it and be nice."

"Can y'all stop being nasty for ten damn minutes so she can get changed? Damn! And your ass better not end up pregnant tonight either."

"Sis stop hatin'. My man said he trying to put another one in you asap."

"The devil is a lie! Girl let's go; your husband trying to start some shit."

Taking the elevator up to their floor, Kiko held onto the train of Orchid's dress until she'd gotten into the room. Standing in the middle of the living room, they passed a blunt while Kiko had to undo more than thirty clasps that held her dress together before she was able to breathe freely.

"Damn that feels good." Orchid said, taking a deep breath.

"Baby D got that ass even more thick than Destiny did. Stop wearing tight shit, maybe your husband won't be up your ass all the time."

"Whatever hater."

"Ain't no 'hateration' here boo. Let me run to the room right quick to get a change of shoes. Don't finish that blunt and get stuck."

"I got this."

Running and hopping into the shower quickly, Orchid stepped out and changed into a knee length, roman inspired reception dress. Stepping into her Jimmy Choo's, she heard the door to her suite open and close.

"It took your ass long enough heffa. Let's go before this nigga puts an APB out on me."

"You're gonna be a little longer than you thought. You should've checked for a pulse bitch!"

True Glory Publications
IF YOU WOULD LIKE TO BE A PART OF OUR
TEAM, PLEASE SEND YOUR SUBMISSIONS BY EMAILTO
TRUEGLORYPUBLICATIONS@GMAIL.COM. PLEASE
INCLUDE A BRIEF BIO, A SYNOPSIS OF THE BOOK, AND
THE FIRST THREE CHAPTERS. SUBMIT USING
MICROSOFT WORD WITH FONT IN 11 TIMES NEW
ROMAN.

Check out these other great books from True Glory Publications

<u>Fetish</u>

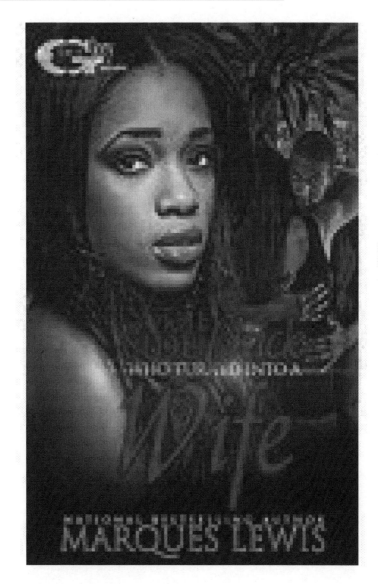

96000634R00072

Made in the USA
Columbia, SC
27 May 2018